An Exceptional
Zephyr

An Exceptional
Zephyr

Dorian Dalta

BALBOA
PRESS

A DIVISION OF HAY HOUSE

Copyright © 2013 Dorian Dalta.

All rights reserved. No part of this book may be used or reproduced by any means, graphic, electronic, or mechanical, including photocopying, recording, taping or by any information storage retrieval system without the written permission of the publisher except in the case of brief quotations embodied in critical articles and reviews.

Balboa Press books may be ordered through booksellers or by contacting:

Balboa Press
A Division of Hay House
1663 Liberty Drive
Bloomington, IN 47403
www.balboapress.com
1-877-407-4847

Because of the dynamic nature of the Internet, any web addresses or links contained in this book may have changed since publication and may no longer be valid. The views expressed in this work are solely those of the author and do not necessarily reflect the views of the publisher, and the publisher hereby disclaims any responsibility for them.

The author of this book does not dispense medical advice or prescribe the use of any technique as a form of treatment for physical, emotional, or medical problems without the advice of a physician, either directly or indirectly. The intent of the author is only to offer information of a general nature to help you in your quest for emotional and spiritual well-being. In the event you use any of the information in this book for yourself, which is your constitutional right, the author and the publisher assume no responsibility for your actions.

Any people depicted in stock imagery provided by Thinkstock are models, and such images are being used for illustrative purposes only. Certain stock imagery © Thinkstock.

Printed in the United States of America.

ISBN: 978-1-4525-8068-5 (sc)
ISBN: 978-1-4525-8070-8 (hc)
ISBN: 978-1-4525-8069-2 (e)

Library of Congress Control Number: 2013915270

Balboa Press rev. date: 9/10/2013

To Chatrapaul Singh.
I miss you, Pops.

Inside a lover's heart
There is another world,
And yet another.

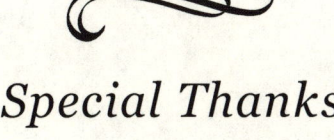

Special Thanks

Mom
Rick
Tyler Jennings
Dawn Johnson
Mark Wolak
Chris and Ruth Laumb
Jon Luhrs
Jesyca Hurd

Chapter 1

What am I afraid of? What have I been so afraid of all these years? Has it all come to this? I've dreaded these moments my whole life. Yet now I am at ease, somehow. Can these two seemingly opposing ruminations share the same space in my mind? I ... I am filled with so much. Where did all the time go? My body hurts. I can no longer breathe freely. My mind is not sharp. But it *is* sharp. It seems as I lie here, I am a surging electrical box of thoughts. They come so easily now. Is it because I have the time? What time? Whose time is it, anyway?

"Who's here?" Did I say that out loud?

"I'm here, Dad," Junior says amiably, although it sounds as though he's distracted.

"I'm here, too; we're all here. What do you need?" Nephew says curtly as he passes.

I know these people. My only son, my nephew, and who is this?

"Can you hear me, Rahja?"

"Ye-es."

"Rahja, I need you to look at me. Can you look at me?"

I think I moved. Yes, my eyes are open. I can move, although it seems through faulty circuits. Oh, this is a nurse. This is a nurse from my doctor's office. Where am I?

"Very good, Rahja; can you see me?" the nurse asks with a soft, direct demeanor.

"Ye-es, but it's blurry."

"That will get better, Rahja. You need to rest. I'm going to leave a list for your nephew."

"What list?" What is she talking about?

"These are a list of your medications, your exercises, and phone numbers in case there is an emergency, okay?"

"Okay."

Okay, yes, I am at home. This is my house. I am lying on my couch. What happened to me? Why do I seem inert or …? Can I feel the weight of my body?

"Time to eat, Dad," Nephew says briskly.

Now what is happening? My nephew is here. Junior is here. What are they doing to me? They're bracing and maneuvering me to an upright position. This feels okay. The TV is on. I can suddenly hear its eternal rambles; now I see its visual display. Junior and Nephew are moving me; they're moving me into a wheelchair. They're helping me stand. They're helping me sit. I can see upright now. Well, this is okay. My body doesn't feel like it is entirely a part of me. I feel heavy and anesthetized. I feel dank and clammy.

Someone is wheeling me to the dining-room table. It's a short trip. There is a large plate of food—chicken curry, rinsed white rice, and steamed mustard greens. I think I can smell it. Oh, what a gift! I love my belly. Everyone must feed and enlighten their belly.

"Junior, is that you?" I can feel someone. No, it's Nephew. Is this a fork? It seems the workings of my body are still relatively functional. The mysteries of my body's mechanisms are still somewhat operable.

"Yeah, there yah go," someone encourages.

"Yeah, Dad, you got it. Have some food now," someone says brusquely.

My mouth suddenly yearns for food. My whole body abruptly yearns for food. My body is awakened in craving and want for nourishment. The first forkful is wonderful, but—*ohhhhhhh, arrrggh*—heaving. I can't catch my breath!

I'll do the service of an explanation. One of my several remedial conditions is known as supranuclear palsy. It's related to Parkinson's disease. Among other things, it creates a situation in which my epiglottis doesn't work properly. In other words, when I swallow, the tap that closes off my airway doesn't always seal properly. Occasionally, specks of chewed food enter my lungs. That's what gets me gasping and coughing when I eat or drink. It also encourages pneumonia. I'll finish my plate anyway. I'll suffer for the pleasure of this wonderful food.

"Take it easy, Dad."

"Take your time now."

"Just a little at a time."

"Slow down now. The food will still be there."

Everyone is always so encouraging. I wonder how much they *really* understand. I just want to clear my plate.

I'm back on the couch now. Oh ... to lie with a full belly. What a precious sensation. I think I'll shut my eyes for a moment. The buzz and ambience of the television is unexpectedly agreeable. Oh to drift in thought ... lazy, meandering thought.

I wonder ...

I wonder what Junior thinks of this. It all seems so unbelievable. So many years lost between us. Where did that time go? I remember when he was a little boy, running with so much energy, smiling with such pure optimism, his perfect little arms and legs chasing around outside under a perfect summer sun. His jet-black hair, his little bowl cut, always with a smile ... my little boy. It all seems to have happened in a flash.

But for most of those years, I wasn't there. How could ten years have gone by—more than ten years? Those lost years. What was Junior doing? What was I doing?

Oh, just to lie here and look at my son—my only son—to look at him now. He's almost forty years old now. To think of how much time has passed in an instant. There he sits, busied by his computer. Such a bright, inquisitive boy he is. His mother did a great job of raising him.

I remember. I remember coming to know his mother. Rose was such a kind-spirited woman, such a wholesome soul. Oh, the sweet sorrow in those memories. How I wish to remember everything, each and every small detail. But such glimmers and reminiscences bring me to sadness. How lovely to recall. I hunger for the heartache of it all— such strange feelings.

Chapter 2

It was in Minnesota. Smack-dab in the middle of North America. It was in Revelation Falls, home of Minnesota State University. It was there I first met Faith, Rose's younger sister. I was beginning my graduate work in biology. A good deal of my time was spent in the university laboratories. They were exquisite facilities compared to those of my motherland, South America. My time in the lab was primarily spent alone, with only the occasional passing of a fellow student or two. Few other students were typically present. Faith was an astonishing exception. She was a striking and tender young blossom, with whom I often had the pleasure of crossing paths. As circumstance granted, we shared a good deal of time together in the labs. Quite naturally, we became acquainted. I was infatuated. I was quite taken with Faith.

She was tall and slender. The contours of her body were simple. Her shapely curves implied symmetry and intricacy. These aspects were continually compelling. She had a classic, timeless beauty. She walked lightly on her feet. Her body remained relaxed as she softly seemed to bounce though space. As our graduate work progressed independently yet side by side, I came to know Faith as sturdy and strong-willed. She had a graceful strength and an intimidating spirit. She was quick and resolute in her opinions and judgments. She was also tolerant and somewhat awkward. The known layers of her disposition were robust. She seemed clear about her bearing and direction. She seemed to know what she was after. The more subtle shades of Faith were guarded. She was often quiet. I never determined if her reticence was a matter of withdrawal or confidence. On certain occasions, she seemed lost and helpless. She held vast depths of unquestioned vulnerability. I could only speculate as to these elements of Faith.

I flirted with her incessantly. I also came to have a great respect for Faith. She was brilliant, with an unwavering ethic toward work. It was fairly clear that nothing of a passionate nature would ever develop between us. Nevertheless, I couldn't help myself. She was a remarkable young woman. There was something about the nature of her chemistry that I was unable to adequately resist. However, she did not allow me to pursue a deeper relationship.

Faith seemed uninterested in my flirtatious advances. She did however seem to take a companionable liking to me. Something in her softness showed a sense of care and concern. Maybe she was curious. I was a foreign student, after all.

Then one day, straight out of nowhere, Faith invited me to her home for dinner. I was tickled. I couldn't believe it. I knew there was little chance of romantic promise, yet I was touched by what seemed to be a genuine show of community and goodwill. As the occasion approached, I learned that she lived with her mother, many siblings, and a retired Catholic priest named Padre Pauly.

I couldn't have prepared for that dinner. I don't think any course of coaching or crash training could have equipped me for the peaks and valleys of what turned out to be a volley of strangeness.

Faith had more than a handful of sisters. Hers was a traditional, large, Catholic family. I was enjoyably staggered. I felt giddy and delightfully uptight. Her family members were all simply and sensually beautiful. They had a clarity that was radically appealing. They were gracious, precociously mannered, and kind. They had a sense of confidence and a misplaced sense of defenselessness that was unfounded … but not far.

To this day, the authority of that memory still seems vividly overwhelming. On entering the simple suburban home, I was battered by a wave of female pheromones. The home also contained a few brothers and Padre Pauly. Even so, a catlike power controlled the place. The appeal of young women frolicking around the house in their tight summer shorts was … well, I could go on and on.

I was welcomed into the living room and adjoining kitchen. The house was busy but quietly so. Undertones of vulnerability and airs of territory were ... I couldn't get a bead on what I was feeling. Maybe American families were much different than what I had expected. My family back home was just as large. Home life in South America was just as busy. Yet in Faith's home, there seemed to be a sense of trepidation or controversy.

Then *she* made her appearance. *She* walked into the room. Looking back, I am thankful that I had been seated. Otherwise, I would have surely second stepped.

Faith's mother approached me directly. She gave me an affable hug and handshake. She welcomed me to both her home and the United States. She carried the conversation with salutation, ceremony, and what only a true artist can do, mesmerizing influence. She guided me from the living room. By the arm, I was led to the dining-room table. There she seated me and then took a seat very closely to mine.

She gazed so thoughtfully, fixing her eyes so deeply into mine. She pulled the proverbial rug of awareness right out from under me. I suddenly became aware of myself again. The conversation went on. She went on. "So I want to hear everything about you. Your people are all so strikingly handsome."

I hadn't uttered a word since she entered the room. She was blatantly conspicuous. I understood more of where Faith came from. The perfection of physical beauty was now shadowed by a much more powerful force of presence. I was shocked by the degree of persuasion she wielded. I was so suddenly daunted.

"Faith tells me you're a brilliant student. These girls," she said, referring to her daughters, who had begun to congregate around the table, "well ... these girls don't understand ... you know ... the finer points or ... sensitive considerations."

She spoke snidely to her daughters and gave me a quick, inclusive wink. It seemed to be a sinister sort of flirtation. She continued to cast a spell with her exposition. "Faith tells me your name is Rahja. What a strong and powerful name. That's the name of a man with purpose and vision. It's biblical. You're a man. You ought to exercise your manhood as you see fit. I'm Victoria. You call me Vicka."

She smiled with the angelic innocence of a saint. Yet her eyes maintained the vibrant spark of a darkened, spoiled force. She was, I sensed, giftedly corrupt. Did I sense something diabolical?

"Will someone get this fine, young gentleman a beer? For the sweet love of Mary, what have you girls been waiting for?" I was encouraged and imbibed a steady flow of domestic American lager that evening, one after another.

The evening eventually attained a degree of traction. I assembled my facilities after a time and was able to share what I hoped was a fair semblance of eloquence and decorum. The conversation grew to one of greater comfort, expression, and concluding entertainment. Our smiles seemed to become more natural as the room relaxed.

Two rather profound events transpired that evening. The first was my acquaintance of Faith's mother, Victoria. The second changed the course of my life forever. It was on this night that I met Junior's mother, my first and only love, my first and only wife. She was one of Faith's older sisters, and her name was Rose.

While Rose had been seated with us the whole time, I only became aware of her as the evening progressed. Padre Pauly, along with six or eight family members, had gathered at the kitchen table. Dinner was served after a time of light but formal conversation.

I'd overlooked Rose until her silence and sense of reserve seemed contrary to its quiet intention. I noticed her by disassociation. I began to watch her on the sly as the conversation continued to chug and rumble around the big family table. Rose's silence began to tell a sort of ominous story about the whole family. Her silence was like a plug that kept the family dysfunction nearly capped. While I could only speculate at that point, the vibrations and waves of engagement were dicey, like cons on the grift.

The constant flow of drink that evening eased the bumps. Nevertheless, I remember the quiver. It shook my nerves. I was haunted when I looked at Rose. The sense of helplessness in her eyes reminded me of a solitary newborn kitten, bashful and stunned. The brief instants of eye contact we shared were like a dark and uncertain path to the bedrock of her emotional dismay. She clearly knew something of darkness. It was a quirk of fate. Vulnerability was the only path to such a degree of human knowing. At the time, it seemed Rose carried the weight of some lost and lonely curse.

The dinner eventually quieted. Family members began to disperse and go about other matters of the evening. Padre Pauly excused himself and said he would retire to his study. Faith and Rose remained at the table, as did Chase and one or two of the other brothers. Another sister may also have been present. The chitchat continued to warm and settle to a degree of relaxed ease and comfort. However, social anxiety still hung in the air. As conversation became better-rounded or inclusive of others, Victoria worked to exert and demonstrate a sense of control and manipulation. She proved to be a master of delivering an array of scathing and lightly sarcastic comments. The strangeness was subtle. It left me wondering if it was really happening. Especially as I was becoming quite influenced by the magnetic persuasion of American lager.

The weirdness persisted. Victoria coaxed me away from the dining-room table. When I stood, I became more directly aware of my inebriated state. She took me by the hand and led me through the kitchen. I looked back dumbly at the dining-room table. Faith, Rose, Chase, and a few others remained seated. Their faces showed a sense of expectation and restrained aversion. Victoria led me into the attached garage by way of an interior kitchen door.

The garage was gloomy and dim, as the evening sun had essentially set for the day. Dark gray shadows were cast from the outside through a small garage window, and another window set in the back garage door. Victoria didn't turn on any lights. I was led by the hand down three stairs from the kitchen door to the concrete garage floor. Turning and facing me, Victoria leaned much of her weight into me. I could feel the heat and succulence of her breath. She closed the kitchen door behind us and renewed her grip on my hand. We continued our path into the darkness of the garage, before stopping under the window along the back wall. There was a makeshift workbench below the window. Some cabinets hung on the wall. I imagined Padre Pauly working there, building a birdhouse or making simple repairs to a lawnmower.

"Here, you stand here. You can lean against this bench," Victoria said with kind directness.

The top of my buttocks were against the workbench. I faced the faint outline of the kitchen door we had just come through. Victoria straddled me. Initially, it felt like an impassioned embrace. Her hips pressed tightly to mine. Her breasts set firmly to my chest. Reflexively, I put my arms around her waist. Her arms, however, did not wrap around my body. Instead, as she continued to lean into me, her arms were busy behind my head. It became apparent that she was rummaging through the cabinets above the bench. I was engulfed by the electricity of her chemistry. She seemed indifferent ... yet available.

"Ahh-huh," she said in affirmation. "Here they are!" She altered the intensity of our superficial embrace by turning slightly to my side. Still, she remained inappropriately close. Some of her weight was now braced against the workbench instead of my body.

"I wanted to come out here and have a cigarette with you." She said, "You *do* smoke don't you? I don't smoke ... but ..." She fished a cigarette from the pack and delicately put it in my mouth. The closeness of our proximity and the inappropriate strangeness of the circumstances were radically appealing.

"I love it when a man smokes," she said as she lit the cigarette hanging from my mouth.

The instant flash and illumination of the stick match were unwelcome. I was relieved to be reenveloped in darkness as my cigarette was lit and the matchstick extinguished. I had been craving a cigarette at moments through dinner but had squashed the thoughts as a matter of simple etiquette. The satiation of this seemingly inconsequential secret with Victoria at this moment awakened other inappropriate and ill-advised desires.

"Oh, I do love the smell of cigarette smoke," Victoria said as she leaned in closely and made a motion to smell my neck.

We shared some moments of silence. I was greatly aroused by the presence of this wonderfully beautiful and stately woman. I was intrigued with countless, hungry possibilities. I was confused. I wasn't of an entirely rational mind. American lager was making a proud and pronounced showing through the channels of my body and mind.

She broke away from our entwined position only to turn and lean back into me. This time, her buttocks were against my hips. She leaned against me as though feigning exhaustion. We remained essentially quiet. My breathing was hurried. I was aroused. I wondered to what degree she could tell. Then, as though responding to the apparent electrochemical charge between us, she said, "Here, feel here." She took my hand and directed it along her stomach. "I think I could lose some weight. What do you think?"

I don't even know if I answered. I moved my hand along her belly and reaffirmed our embrace. She seemed to reciprocate. It was strange, seductive, and intentionally sinister. It was intoxicating. It was dreadfully alluring.

By then my smoke was done. Quietly and with motherly regard, Victoria took the cigarette from my mouth. She threw it to the garage floor and rolled it under the ball of her elegantly shod foot. She took my hand again and led us back to the kitchen door. At the three steps leading back up to the kitchen door she stopped. She turned toward me. It was dark, yet I could see that she was gazing intently into my eyes.

FROM THE DIARY OF ROSE …
June 14, 1970

Oh my gosh!! What a night!! I don't want to forget this night!! Faith brought a boy home, a boy she met from school. His name is Rahja. He's a foreign student from somewhere in South America I think. He was so worldly. He told such entrancing stories. He was so handsome. Ohh, he was sooo dashing. Faith said they were just friends. I think they have class together … or work in the labs or something. Oh I probably made a fool of myself. I didn't say anything. I should have said something … ANYTHING!! But my mom!! She would have ruined it. She DID ruin it!! I think Rahja kept looking at me. Oh I don't know?! Oh my mom!! She embarrassed us all. I have to get away!! I can't believe I still live at home. I'm almost 21 yrs old. My mom just laughs at us. I hope I get to see Rahja again!! I am so…I feel silly!! I feel crazy!! I am cast in a spell…a magical spell!!!…a spell of love…my insides feel like they're laughing all over…

Chapter 3

Chase felt light and spry. He was energized. The high-grade cocaine now coursing through his system had him full of fancy. He was confident, but not with malice or ill intent. He cackled with fun and a sense of innocent frolic. Regrettably, the growing number of police cars trailing him were likely not of the same light and smiling friskiness. This had very quickly turned into a high-speed police pursuit. Sirens blaring, the sharp squeal of radial tires, the smell of gasoline and hardened road dust; this had all the makings of an overblown media fanfare. Just the same, this wasn't Southern California; this was Revelation Falls. While it may show up late on the local news broadcast or the third page of the local newspaper, this was not national news. This was Revelation Falls. Behind the steering wheel, Chase veered sharply and laughed as he turned up the radio.

Onlookers gawked with a bit of alarm but mostly with surprise. While they may have shook their fists in the air or grimaced, they were more likely excited by the sense of adventure. Revelation Falls wasn't a small town, but it wasn't so large that one could drift into the crowd of anonymity. There was a sense of safety and community interwoven between the residents and their city. Some of the onlookers probably knew of Chase or his family.

Chase cranked the steering wheel. His car slid awkwardly around a corner and sputtered. He feathered the accelerator and prevented the car from fully stalling out. Once some smoke cleared, he realized the car had spun. He was facing the downtown barbershop. He and his car sat directly in front of the slowly revolving barbershop marquee. For reasons unknown, the capsule-shaped pergola cast him awestruck. He watched the spinning capsule. He watched the revolving red ribbon. He pondered. He watched as the revolving red stripe seemed to rotate in ascent. He realized an interesting notion. No matter what angle it was viewed from, the twirling barbershop marquee was never fully visible. Yet the red ribbon was always connected. The red spinning ribbon was one rising line.

The appearance of a person startled Chase. From behind the barbershop glass, the barber stood, watching Chase. Chase sat behind the wheel of the jalopy, watching the barber. He thought, *How strange and curious*. The barber had a striking similarity to Padre Pauly.

The blare of approaching police sirens awoke him from his rumination. He checked the rearview mirror, smiled, and slammed the accelerator to the floor. The pursuit resumed.

The game of tag between Chase and the law enforcement officials of Revelation Falls kept going around the same small section of the city. Locals knew the area as the ring road. It encircled the downtown shopping district and encompassed twelve or fifteen city blocks. It was an older section of town but remained somewhat viable for local business. Old granite, limestone, and brick structures of two or three stories from more than a century ago housed various shops of contemporary products and services. The ring road was joined with dramatically oversized portions of pedestrian concrete. People milling from shop to shop didn't have to contend with much vehicle traffic. Sitting areas and statues and play structures for children were scattered about the pedestrian parts of the ring road. Provided the high-speed police pursuit stayed on the road, onlookers were afforded a safe distance from which to observe the entertaining mishap happenings.

More police cruisers joined the pursuit. Because the car chase appeared to be covering the same course, law enforcement began considering the possibility of a roadblock. They knew Chase and his disconcerting shenanigans. They hoped he was sensible enough to play by some semblance of rules, if for no other reason than the safety of innocent bystanders.

Chase made another round of the ring road. The pursuing police cruisers were gaining on him but keeping a reasonable distance. They were waiting for further instructions regarding how aggressively to proceed.

Chase rounded a corner and was again captivated by the spinning barbershop marquee. He didn't stop his car this time, but he slowed long enough to get a good look at the spinning red ribbon display and the barber behind the large glass window. He couldn't shake those images or the growing sense of ... but what was it? What was he doing? He looked in the rearview mirror at the radiant blink of red and blueberry lights. Was the cocaine wearing off? He hit the gas pedal hard, but this time without the same sense of conviction.

That barbershop display held a message for Chase. He knew it. That spinning red ribbon was trying to tell him something. The inexplicable was almost completely mysterious, yet simply and easily attainable. Yes! That was it. Was the red spinning ribbon like God? Was this a religious thing? Was this a spiritual thing? Was this the cocaine talking? He knew a metaphor was staring him in the face. He knew quite easily what it was. Yet he wasn't ready to acknowledge the simplicity of it all. It was as though a grand life lesson had just slapped him in the face. Perhaps he'd been given the most important message he would ever glimpse. Was that it? Was that humanity's simple and entwined relationship with God? *Holy shit*, he thought, *I'm going to need to give this a good deal more thought ... humanity, the spinning white capsule ... God, the ascending red ribbon that can never be fully seen ... but always connected ... always there ... but ...*

Chase was all at once bored, restless, and agitated. He was again rounding the corner where the barbershop stood; the same spinning marquee ... the same gentleman behind the large glass windowpane. Police cruisers had set up a makeshift roadblock further up the street, but Chase didn't bother to go that far. He came to a screeching halt on the sidewalk in front of the barbershop, his car not more than itches away from the large glass window. The barber who had a striking resemblance to Padre Pauly did not appear to be alarmed at Chase's impulsive actions.

Chase casually exited the stolen jalopy and walked toward the spinning barbershop marquee. Once in front of it, he stood and looked on, mesmerized. He couldn't get over it. He'd been seeing these twirling barbershop marquees since he was a kid. He'd never given them a second thought beyond their initial discovery. Now he couldn't believe he'd overlooked such a powerful and cataclysmic metaphor. He was especially struck by the encompassing thick, red ribbon. The cherry-colored line wound up indefinitely. It was but one single line; a red line you could never see in it's entirely. The line was broken by the circumference on which it spun. It was a metaphor for all that was mysterious. It was a metaphor for God.

Chase was tremendously dumbfounded. The barber with the striking resemblance to Padre Pauly came into view through the window. All at once Chase was reminded of his family. He thought of his crazy mother, Victoria. He thought of his sisters. While they were all within hold of his mental grasp, he thought especially of Faith, Grace, and Rose—sweet, innocent Rose, who so quietly carried the weight of the family's sensitivities and pathology. Chase felt a heavy lump in his throat. His chin began to quiver. His vision blurred as tears filled his eyes.

The spinning barbershop marquee was blotted abruptly from Chase's view. He realized he'd been tackled by cops. All the noise and commotion of a busy daytime street returned to his senses. His body began to ache at being thrust to the pavement so vigorously. The cocaine was wearing off, and he yearned so badly for more. The reality of what he'd done surfaced clearly in his brain. He'd stolen a car and gone on a tame joyride. He should have ditched the car sooner. He should not have gotten into a chase with cops. He already had a string of similar offenses. The cops liked Chase. They knew that in his heart he was a good kid. But the law is the law; this time he'd be going to prison. But it didn't seem to matter. Chase had learned some sort of life-changing lesson. He didn't quite know what it was. He was going to need some time to think about it, and now he'd have all the time he needed.

Chapter 4

Padre Pauly was on the upper terrace of the rectory. He was alone in a mostly quiet, slumbering night. In the distance, he heard a young woman singing through expansive silence. Her voice innocently cut through the darkness. She was off-key with little regard to rhythmic cadence or melodic sensibilities. Yet her voice had such purity and simple virtuosity. Padre Pauly smiled. By the sound of her sweet vocalizations and the early morning hour, it was likely the young woman was returning from town after a night of a few too many drinks.

Padre Pauly's smile faded as he looked down at his hands. In one, a cigarette; in the other, a thick glass tumbler. The ice in the tumbler had begun to melt. It was nearly empty of its sharp amber essence. The ice jangled as Padre Pauly tipped the glass to his mouth and drained the whiskey. The sky contained a few jeweled speckles of starlight. He kept looking, his mind swimming with a balance of possibilities. He remembered the wonders and philosophic potential of this wonderful beverage. This was the young man's first independent, unsupervised assignment as a Catholic priest. It was nighttime in the little northern town of Morningstar. In fact, it was well past midnight.

He smiled, but not without deliberation or repentance. A woman was cozily nestled in his bed, a woman from his small-town congregation, a woman of his flock ... a married woman named Victoria.

Padre Pauly greedily took the last pull from his cigarette, little more than a remnant of filter. The filter softened between his fingertips. The last pull was hot in his mouth, and he winced slightly at the potential of burning his lips and tongue. He exhaled with a huff and snuffed out the cigarette. He took one last look at the sky. His eyes fell to the church steeple and the rooftops of this rural community. He could see the mercantile store and some of the other main street shops. He could also see a dozen or so of the town's quaint homes. His ponderings were richly optimistic. He felt especially good, light. Perhaps this buoyant confidence was little more than the result of the whiskey flowing through his veins.

He left the terrace and reentered the three-story rectory by way of the partly open French doors. Light, silken curtains swayed indolently as he passed. The bedroom was mostly darkened, obscure shades of blackened and dark gray objects. Nevertheless, his eyes were mostly adjusted to the darkness. What his eyes lacked of sight, his other senses accommodated.

He could hear her long, relaxed breathing. He could smell her soft, sun-dappled skin. He could hear her move slightly in his bed. She wasn't sleeping. She could sense him, too. He sat next to her as she remained lying in bed. He put his arm on her shoulder. He could see the sparkling glint in her eyes through the darkness of the room. He felt such warmth run through his trunk and dance to the tips of his fingers and toes.

"How are you, my darling?" he asked.

"Oh Pauly, that is not something you have to ask, and you know it," Victoria said sweetly but with what seemed a hint of venom.

Pauly shed his clothes and slipped into bed next to Victoria. She was also naked. While an energetic bout of lovemaking had already occurred, it seemed they were both ready again. Before reengaging in the entirely natural, Pauly felt constrained by the crossroads of contradiction. It seemed the pit of irony. His rudimentary and foundational Catholic education gave him a dreadful feeling of guilt. But his flesh and breathing humanity flexed with vibrancy and flashing electricity.

"Victoria, we, I ... where are we, or ... can we keep on like this?"

"Oh Pauly," Victoria began as she tightened and pulled away, only slightly, "who are we to deny ..." She put her leg between his, but pulled her bare-breasted chest from his. "Pauly, we love each other." Then she seemed to shift gears, as though a series of thoughts were beginning to occur to her. "Well, maybe I'll just leave then." She sat up in bed and began to rummage for her discarded clothes. She smiled.

"Vicka, I don't mean ... I'm not trying to ... I just feel terrible about—"

"What do you mean you feel terrible? How could you? Do you love me?"

"Vicka, you know. It's just that, well, you're a married woman, with children."

"Pauly," she began, her smile fading into something more strongly serious, "maybe we just need to end this, then. Is that what you want? I can tell my husband, and you can tell the bishop. We can just come clean and forget all this."

A sense of dread struck Pauly in the pit of his stomach and the front lobe of his brain. "Vicka, don't leave like this." His mind swimming, he struggled to grasp the thread of events that seemed to be slipping away. How had things changed so quickly?

Vicka stood naked before the French-style doors. Her stance was uncomplicated and firm. He could see her white skin was perceptibly soft even through the distance that separated them. Her essence gave off an indefinable light through the darkened room. She was simply and altogether beautiful, stately and traditionally feminine. Something pure and eternal exuded from her. She paused as if displaying herself, innocently, like a schoolgirl. God created this beauty, which struck Padre Pauly so powerfully. This was surely a test. Was he at peace with the beauty of God's creation? Could he accept such beauty?

"Come back to bed, Vicka. Let's try to ..." Pauly was terribly conflicted. His normally unwavering moral compass was losing to his biochemical urge to engage in physical companionship.

"Oh Pauly, honey," she said, returning to the bed. She sat next to Pauly, who was now lying down. "I can't stay. Stanley is probably passed out, but the kids will be up soon. I have to be home for that." She rubbed his chest. Then she reached between his legs. She began to stroke with a tacit sense of dominance. She looked in his eyes and then kissed him on the lips. "I have to go, Pauly, we have to ... I don't know."

"Vicka, my dear."

"I have to go, Pauly."

In only moments she was gone, leaving the silken curtain swaying. Padre Pauly was left to a blurred flurry of ruminations. He had Sunday morning mass to conduct in a few hours. Victoria and her large family would be there. Most of Morningstar would be there. Nevertheless, he thought not of his erroneous path. He thought not of mending his ways with Victoria's husband, Stanley. He thought not of restoring his ways with the bishop. Instead, he thought about how he had come to know Victoria.

Chapter 5

"Dad ... Dad ... are you sleeping? Are you sleeping, Dad?"

"Wha? No ... no ... just thinking."

"Time to take your pills. Time to take your pills, Dad."

"Okay."

Nephew is before me with a clear cough medicine cup of multicolored pills. There must be a dozen pills there. The different shapes and sizes strike me as a three-dimensional, animated collage. I mouth the pills and slug them down with water. I cough and sputter. But the pills make their way down my gullet.

The house is quiet. I'm lying on the couch. I'm positioned before the picture window in the living room. It overlooks my three-season porch and the chain-link fence that surrounds my tiny urban yard. It is evening now. It doesn't seem especially late, as a fair deal of traffic still proceeds outside.

"Dad, I gotta hit the trail. I gotta get back home ... it's a long drive," Junior offers.

"Okay. Or you just stay the night." I feel a stab of affecting dismay and loneliness in hearing of Junior's departure.

"Ah Dad, I'll be back soon. Make sure ... uh ... take your time ... listen to Nephew, and do all the exercises from the doctor."

"Okay." I only want to be Junior's daddy again. Will we ever recover all those lost years?

As Junior makes his final preparations for departure, he quietly talks with Nephew by the front door. It is near where I lie on the couch. Are they whispering? Are they talking about me? They both go outside. I can see that they're smoking. I can see that they're conversing. The nature of their conversation doesn't seem to be especially serious. But it does seem to take a certain tone, a tone I am unable to fully discriminate.

Junior drives off. Nephew comes back into the house. He brings a fresh waft of outside air with him. The refreshing air has a twinge of cigarette smoke. It is a wonderful combination of scents. He also brings a dark loneliness with him. I know it's not his fault, but I feel a weight of sadness that seems to accompany him. It seems to happen all at once. It feels like a dire Sunday evening for the workingman.

Nephew proceeds to the kitchen and instigates a quiet ruckus. Maybe he's cooking or washing dishes. Nephew is a wonderful cook and a proficiently viable homemaker. Now he passes through the main floor hallway and hurries up the staircase, two steps at a time. From my position on the couch, I have a good vantage point of the main living areas of my home, except the back porch, kitchen, and main floor hallway.

Nephew moves promptly back downstairs with a load of laundry. He goes back through the main floor hallway and down the basement stairs to the washing machine and dryer. Soon he is back up the stairs and in the kitchen for another bout of domestic industry.

Nephew is certainly good to me. It is good to have someone here with me. Am I selfish? Am I taking advantage of Nephew? He lives and cares for me here in my home. He initially came from South America—our Motherland. He came in an effort to secure citizenship here in the United States of America. Now his visa has expired. I suppose that makes him an illegal resident. I know he's still working on it. He serves me well.

His timing could only have been heaven sent. His arrival to my home, almost five years ago, came at a time when I was rather sick. I was suffering some complications related to my second heart attack. With his arrival, I was able to come home early from the hospital.

I have endured countless hospital stays since then. They often entail some temporary stay in a nursing home, aimed at rehabilitation. I go to the nursing home to gain back my strength. I've always been able to come home on account of Nephew's presence. Time and events have shown me that I can no longer live on my own.

Have I become a burden? Sometimes I am struck with such a distressful sense of grief. Nephew has a wife and two children back in South America. But isn't this what a family does for one of its own? Isn't this what service is about? Nursing homes don't exist in my small village. Families care for elders in their homes. It's considered a great honor to care for one's elders. Would Junior come to live with me? Would Junior care for me? I wish he would. Could forgiveness mend our wounds? Whose forgiveness? Whose wounds? Are all those years—all those lost years between Junior and me—too wide a gap? Those ten years ... lost.

Nephew comes to the living room and sits on the adjacent sofa. He grabs the remote control for the television from the coffee table. He changes the channel to a crime scene investigation program. It must be prime time in the evening.

He looks at me. I can see his movements in my periphery. I surmise he is gathering whether I am awake or asleep. I am awake. We watch the program together for a while.

"I have to pee," I say.

"Okay," Nephew says, with a slightly bothered sense of compliance. He helps me into the wheelchair as he keeps his eyes focused on the television program. He wheels me to the small bathroom in the main floor hallway. He helps me stand.

"I have to poop," I say.

"All right."

He takes my hand. Then he takes my arm. Then he helps me turn around.

"There, Dad, there. With your left hand, grab onto the brace. There, with your left hand, grab the brace to help lower yourself." Nephew speaks with a repetitive sense of urgency. "No, wait!"

Nephew lowers my pants before I sit. After I finish pooping, Nephew makes certain I am clean. He pulls my pants back up.

I begin to cry. I don't blubber. I just cry.

"You okay, Dad? Why do you cry, Dad?"

"I don't know ... so many things. This ... an ... and Junior ... and your wife and kids and ... just so many things."

"Ah, Dad, don't worry."

"Yeah."

Nephew helps me back into the wheelchair. We make the short trip back into the living room. He helps me back to the couch. He fluffs my pillows and braces me up. He smells like perspiration and dish soap. He smells like curry powder and cologne.

We continue to watch the crime scene investigation program. I look out the living room picture window. The large parking lot and adjoining business bustle with mid-evening activity. The businesses and surrounding community have changed over the years. My neighborhood is now primarily comprised of Hmong people. I'm not Hmong. I am an East Indian.

Having cried, my mind is blank. I'm tired. I'm emotionally subdued.

Rose enters my mind again; my first and only wife, the mother of my first and only child, Junior. Unsettled thoughts of Rose begin making a presence in my mind. I am not able to gather their message. They're only flashes and glimmers of faded memories, bouncing around unattached.

A Poem from Rahja to Rose:

Some like them look, some like them sold
Some like them when they are not too darn old
Some like them fat, some like them lean
Some like them only at sweet sixteen
Some like them darker, some like them light
Some like them in the park, late at night
Some like them fickle some like them true
But the way I like them, is when they're like you...

"I want to go to bed," I say. I want to be alone with my thoughts.

"Okay Dad. Are you okay, Dad?"

"Yes."

Nephew helps me into the wheelchair and wheels me into the small dining room. I have a bedroom on the second floor of my house. However, stair climbing is no longer advised. I can't use my own bedroom anymore. It has become obsolete. Instead, a small bed has been placed in my dining room. It's at the opposite end of my house from where my couch sits, opposite the picture window in the living room, opposite where I lie during the day.

Nephew helps me out of the wheelchair. He sits me on the bed. He helps me out of my clothes. He puts me in a disposable overnight undergarment. He lays me down. He covers me with a white sheet and a soft blanket. The blanket has a silky edge that is enticingly soft to the touch.

"Night, Dad."

"Good night, son," I say through the opening of grateful tears.

It occurs to me that I've just referred to Nephew as my son. Nephew also calls me Dad. I wonder when this started. I guess it's just become natural to me. It's our habit now. It doesn't require belabored deliberation. Perhaps we've been referring to each other this way for a long time now. I can't say for sure.

Nephew goes back to the sofa to resume his television program. I can see him from where I lie. I don't look at him. I close my eyes and let my thoughts drift back to Rose.

Chapter 6

He'd noticed Victoria straight away. His congregation in Morningstar, his very first congregation, was smallish but not so small that the faces of his flock couldn't get lost in the sea of features and expressions. She seemed so all at once apparent. Victoria's face always burst out from that sea of nondescript faces. Victoria had several children. Their faces, too, seemed especially vibrant, especially noteworthy. Even the face of her husband, Stanley, had certain outstanding qualities.

Padre Pauly looked forward to seeing their faces on Sunday mornings. But he especially hoped to see Victoria. He looked forward to it more than he would likely admit. Something about her was marvelous. Her distinctive qualities seemed to mingle in a way that was a bit beyond explanation. She moved with such poise. She carried herself with such grace. While most indications suggested she was a typical housewife with a large family, there seemed to be another collection of attributes that were far from typical. She harbored depth. She harbored an unknowable abyss that simply demanded knowing. Didn't anyone else sense that? Who was this woman?

As Padre Pauly conducted his Sunday morning church service, he stole glances at Victoria and her family. When he looked at her, she always seemed so captivated by his words. She seemed utterly enraptured by his pious dissertations.

Padre Pauly also conducted a weekday mass on Wednesday mornings. These gatherings were subject to the season, as Morningstar was a rural farming community. By the level of attention and dedication Victoria gave to Sunday mass, Padre Pauly was always surprised to never see Victoria during these weekday gatherings.

Nevertheless, Victoria was always present at confession. These were intermittently scheduled but typically occurred twice every month. It was during these meetings that Padre Pauly truly began to fall. His religious, professional, and other measures of bearing were becoming skewed. Victoria bared her heart. She bared her private sensitivities. She opened her spirituality to Pauly. She too had fallen. Padre Pauly and Victoria fell toward one another.

Victoria spoke of a harrowing home life. She spoke of how difficult it was to have ten children in her home, many quite young. She spoke of a kind but nonexistent husband. Apparently, Stanley was a man who worked, slept, and drank. Pauly was engrossed. Victoria's tears were sweet and painful. Her convictions and aspirations were divine. Padre Pauly was drawn so completely by the vigor and allure of this woman. She was hurting and wounded. She was one of God's very own.

Was Padre Pauly responsible? Did God put Victoria in his path for a reason? Padre Pauly couldn't help but think such events were most certainly of heavenly intercession. Yes, of course! That was it! It was he who was most certainly responsible. How could he deny one of God's own? One who was hurt and wounded. One who is in need of intervention.

After a relatively easy course to deliberation, Padre Pauly resolved to hire Victoria. He'd provide her with simple purpose. He'd renew her path to one that included an occupation outside her debilitating home. He'd provide her with a sense of independence, a sense of purpose. He'd provide her with a modest paycheck. What could be better? It seemed so logical. The church in Morningstar had yet to solidify its music program. Padre Pauly would appoint Victoria as the church organist.

Their relationship grew exponentially from this point. It was only natural. They became allies. Their association became much more tightly knit. As such, it was only normal that they meet in the church rectory. After all, they had things to discuss. They had a reason. They had a path. They had business to attend to, church business.

They were careful. Victoria and Padre Pauly were very careful. They were aware of what others might observe.

They were acutely aware. They were aware of the obvious nuance that flowed between them. They began to play with the undercurrent. Often it was an effortless touch from one another. Sometimes it was an extra moment of eye contact. They liked the sharing. They liked that it was exclusive. Was it wrong? No, heaven's no. They were just well connected. They were developing history. They began to mock anyone who opposed their friendship. Why should anyone have a problem with them? The problem was more likely jealousy and envy, wasn't it? Their mockery of the outside world propelled and deepened their connection. And, of course, why wouldn't it?

Then one evening it changed. Their relationship changed. It was a simple and sealed kiss. But it was more complicated than that. Wasn't it?

Chapter 7

After the dinner debacle at the home of Faith's family, things settled back to normal student life. Faith and I continued to work in the lab. We conversed lightly and playfully among the beakers, vials, and Bunsen burners. The days passed uneventfully.

One change did occur. Rose began making a presence. She would accompany Faith to class or pick her up when class was over. The same sense of soft vulnerability was present in her eyes. Her demeanor was shy and submissive. She didn't say much, but it seemed clear she wished to be included. Rose emanated a whole sense of loneliness. She was quiet and apparently kind. Her eyes held a profound sense of anxious longing. The openness or exposure in her gaze wasn't a weakness. It struck me curiously. She had a sort of strength. I was drawn to Rose—to that sense of strength—in ways I couldn't fully explain. I still can't really explain it. I wanted to provide her with something, like safekeeping. I was uncontrollably inquisitive. Perhaps it was her hidden strength I was drawn to. She had a depth, a depth so seemingly unique yet so plainly attainable. Her doors were open to me. Knowingly or not, I was becoming cast in a spell, a spell of breathless enchantment.

Our relationship began simply enough. We finagled small talk while she waited for or departed from Faith. Rose was also a student at the state university in Revelation Falls. Our conversations seemed to grow naturally. We were soon arranging coffee and other simple outings. We seemed to have more and more to share with each other.

I felt like a rascal or a lazybones. My motivations seemed dastardly. While Rose wasn't blatantly feeble or fragile, she had a real need for understanding and connection. Perhaps these were things she'd never had. Did I take advantage of Rose? I knew how to fulfill her needs. I'm sure there were many things about each of us that interested the other. We were like moths, flying around each other's lightbulb. While I didn't realize it then, I realize it now; I had something like the inverse of her needs. Ours was a sharpened lock and key fit.

The state university in Revelation Falls is built along the Mississippi River, the famous river that essentially transects the United States from east and west. I always thought it dramatically profound that I should be so privileged as to study along its steady and notable flow.

Rose and I used to steal away and engage in naked, hurried mischief along its banks. We seemed to have only begun. Our affinity toward one another seemed to spiral, twist, and coil right out of control. It was as though we'd been flung. Everything happened so quickly.

<p style="text-align:center">I drank a lot.
~~~ I drank too much. ~~~
I drank for too many years.</p>

I graduated from the state university and moved from Revelation Falls. I moved to the metropolitan city of New Providence. New Providence lies about an hour west of Revelation Falls. Mostly, I liked the space I was afforded from Rose. However, the distance from her made for a deeper and more piercing sense of being alone. I felt guilty. I felt like I'd left Rose behind. Her home life, mother, and siblings were powerfully difficult for her. I had been an island for her; I'd offered a sense of sanctuary during some difficult times. Now I'd left her. Had I abandoned her?

I was struggling with my own inner demons. I was struggling with a painfully uncompromising outer world. At times, I was struggling something fierce. I wasn't yet a US citizen. I was having a horribly difficult time finding work. On good days, I felt strong in my independence and isolation from Rose. On bad days, I was dreadfully insecure, lost, and lonely, with little hope. Rose was someone I knew I could lean on. In those times, I took advantage of her. I knew it. I needed to. I needed her. I needed Rose.

She began coming to New Providence. She took the bus. It was sad somehow ... some kind of a lone voyage to make contact briefly, only to say good-bye. The sadness of it all was so strangely magnificent. Rose was so good. She was so good to me. She tended to me so simply and thoughtfully. She worked so hard to make good food. She brought me a secondhand knit sweater once when the weather turned cold.

Oh, how we began to make love! We were both so desperate. We latched onto each other, because we were scared. We were unsure of ourselves. Maybe we were looking for certainty in the other. We didn't know any better. We were doing the only thing that seemed directly natural. We were doing the only thing we knew for safety or connection.

FROM THE DIARY OF ROSE
September 19, 1970

I don't know what's happening. I am so confused. I am in love with Rahja. I think he's in love with me too. I hope he really loves me. How could he possibly love me? I think Rahja has a drinking problem. I don't know ... maybe not ... I don't know. Padre Pauly used to have a drinking problem, but he quit. My mom told me not to see Rahja anymore. I think she's jealous. It's so weird!! I don't know what I am doing. But Rahja is ... he is so amazing. We snuck away. We made love by the river. It was so simple. It just happened. It wasn't like I thought it would be, but it all just happened. It just happened all by itself. He's so passionate. He's going to sweep me up. He's going to take me away from here.

~~~ The drinking made it easier. ~~~
The drinking eased the jolts.
The drinking was a problem.

Rose came to New Providence for Valentine's Day. We just stayed in bed. It was wonderful, simple. The world went away, yet our purpose for living seemed all the more clear. I was especially saddened with her departure on that occasion. But I remember feeling a keen, clear sense of elation. I don't know why. I don't think I ever shared that with Rose. I came to understand later. It was on this occasion that Junior was conceived.

My subconscious is better aware of how things transpired from that point. My conscious memory was not particularly reliable. The drinking kept a general fog over the happenings of that period. I was pretty well pummeled most of the time. I came to know that Rose was pregnant. The failings of my recollections are such that I forget the specifics of how I came to know. Did Rose call and initially inform me of the news over the phone? Did she tell me in person? Did I somehow know intuitively? I don't remember.

Rose didn't visit often. We were both burdened in several ways; money was no exception. The bus trip, while reasonable, was a considerable expense for each of us. But even though we saw little of each other, I knew a world of change was making earth-rumbling conversions. Fissures were appearing. Walls were caving. I was still looking for work. Pressure was mounting. What was I going to do? I was lost. I was lonely. I was a very long way from my home country. How was all this happening?

Drinking helped.
~~~   Drinking knew my pain.   ~~~</center>

> Drinking was just the friend I needed.
> Drinking so personally understood me.

I found myself more frequently returning to Revelation Falls, where Rose was still a student. I had no job. I had no real associates in New Providence. I had a few cousins and brothers who were also attending the state university in Revelation Falls. My charming sense of persuasion landed me a temporary room in a home dedicated to foreign students. When I wasn't at the state university in Revelation Falls, I was in New Providence. What was I doing with my time? I cannot recall clearly. Some things remain so deeply etched in my memory. Some things drift as nothing more than haunting undertones or rumors of my mind. So much was happening. It may as well have been a tornado. I wouldn't have known the difference. Was it a dream? Am I dreaming now? The demarcation of either seems indiscernible sometimes.

> **FROM THE DIARY OF ROSE**
> **April 5, 1971**
>
> ---
>
> I'm pregnant. I'm pregnant!! I'm pregnant!!! I told Rahja. I don't know what he thinks. I thought he would be excited. I'm scared too!! But I thought... I thought this could bring us together. I am so scared. No one knows. I have to tell someone. I'll tell my sister Grace. She'll know what to do. Maybe Rahja will just run away now. I think Rahja has a drinking problem. All his brothers and cousins drink a lot, too. Maybe it's part of Rahja's culture. Maybe it has to do with how he was raised. I want to be with Rahja. I think Rahja wants to be with me too. I'm excited too. I just want to be close to Rahja. Maybe he'll just hold me. That would be good enough. If we can just be close... Then I won't feel so all alone.

Rose was pregnant. It hardly seemed real. How does—how did—that happen?

Maybe the pregnancy drew me back to her. Maybe that's why I settled back to Rose. Maybe that's why I stayed in Revelation Falls more often. The trajectory of my aim was not certain.

Rose began spending more time with me in my temporary room in Revelation Falls. She was still a student at the state university and on campus nearly every day. I was torn to pieces. I knew I could love Rose. That part was easy. But I didn't know how to do it. Did Rose cage me in? I felt I was under a heavy, wet blanket. I couldn't move. I felt inevitable asphyxiation.

Oh, the excruciating sense of guilt. Rose tried to tell me. She tried to include me. She wanted me to be a part of her. She gave. She surrendered. She just wanted to be acknowledged. She just wanted a simple gesture of recognition. She accepted my baby in her belly.

I drank.
~~~ I just kept drinking. ~~~

</div>

I remember the hangover of one particular morning. It still strikes me as a frightful apparition. Not to say hangovers were anything unusual at that time. However, the menacing vibrations of that particular morning were a brand of darkness I had not yet experienced or known. Rose was up early. She was always an early morning riser. I remember her whispers.

"I'm bleeding. I'm bleeding a lot." Her demeanor was calm and serious, pressured, and sensibly pragmatic. "I'm ... I've got to call the doctor. Is this a ... miscarriage? This seems like an awful lot of blood."

I was frozen. I was sick. I was all but in a panic. I was emotionally fevered. My stomach cast spasms of knots. My skin emanated rancid sweat.

"I've got to go, Rahja. The doctor said to come right away. Rahja, honey?"

I stayed. I just stayed in bed. I know not what I said. I gave some well-spoken, indefensible excuse. I curled into a pale ball and remained in bed.

She walked to the doctor's office, with Junior in her belly, the mother of my child. She walked to the doctor's office. She walked. She could have walked herself into a miscarriage.

―•―

Rose was ordered to bed rest. If she wasn't in school or at her family residence, she came to my temporary room and rested. Some kind of calm happened to me during this period. Maybe I felt guilty. Maybe I felt grateful. I can't say for sure.

After the passage of a strange period of timelessness, as though ordained by someone in the Watchtower, Rose showed up at my door. She was accompanied by her older sister, Grace. The tone was dire. Yet there was a poised sense of hope. There was a practical sense of dignity and heart. They had a plan. They ensured justice and honor were upheld. After all, this is what human beings do for one another. Their plan was comprehensive. A realignment of righteousness took place.

Rose and I were married June 9, 1971. I just showed up to the church at the appointed time. I wonder if they thought I'd skip out. Could I have done that?

My pal at the time had a car. From the wedding, he drove us to the small town of Luck. Luck stood two hours by car from New Providence and one hour from Revelation Falls. The locality of each was positioned in a sort of slanted line when viewed on a map.

We needed a clean start.

Chapter 8

A tangible line had formally been crossed between the two of them. A kiss. A kiss on the lips.

Pauly was not any sort of simpleton. Leading his first Catholic parish, he was a mature young man. Padre Pauly was a man not without sophisticated experiences. Just the same, Pauly was an alcoholic. Even so, he was also a man who lived by a deep-rooted sense of principle. He was a man of disciplined conviction.

The kiss he and Victoria shared marked a signpost. The kiss was a cherry-red siren, indicating treacherous roads ahead. Was this a problem with more than just curiosity?

Padre Pauly and Victoria had met on a Saturday evening. The plan was to review music for Sunday mass the following morning. Victoria arrived after 9 p.m. Pauly had consumed a bit more than his usual allotment of iced amber whiskey but was still within the range of respectable and acceptable limits. Victoria brought a small bottle of wine, which had become a more common occurrence. Stanley was working at the local bar. Victoria's children were either in bed or soon to be.

"Oh, Pauly, I have a beautiful song to share with you this evening. Just one before we move to the music for tomorrow morning." Victoria was already seated at the piano with an innocently playful smile.

Pauly was caught in a moment. It was thick. She sat so wonderfully. How could she have bore ten children and remained this youthful and fit. She was slender. She was still young. She was apparently fit and supple. She sat poised lightly atop the piano bench. She had such class, such mannered decorum.

"You okay, Pauly? Cat got your tongue?" she asked, smiling.

Pauly knew they'd been treading upon inappropriate territory with each other for some time. While no real physical contact had taken place, the amount of time they spent together and its frequency were certainly questionable. People were no doubt talking about it. It was only a matter of time before that accusatory conversation came knocking on his door.

She began to sing. Time seemed to sort of joggle and hitch. She played and sang like a sweet and unassuming songbird. She sang like an angel. It was a quaint piano ballad from the 1930s. The melody she sang was light and sad. The syncopated piano in the chorus sections tinkled like raindrops just beginning to form. Pauly loved classic and contemporary piano renditions. Victoria was gifted. Pauly was lost. His bearing in the presence of Victoria had been slipping for some time. Enraptured in song, it was difficult to maintain any sort of stable comportment. The root of his difficulty was bound in internal questions. *Why am I in the presence of such beauty and charm? Why is God doing this to me? What question does the universe insist on keeping from me?*

Victoria finished. She, too, had become caught in the atmosphere of her song. They were quiet. The mood lingered, still caught on the wings of the lasting melodies.

"Can I pour you a small glass of wine, Padre?" Victoria asked in a reserved, serious way. The tone of her voice was dry, suggesting the wine was a mere formality.

"Certainly," Pauly started. "Victoria you sing wonderfully."

"Thank you, Pauly. I ... I guess I really love it. I forget about beauty sometimes. You know? Simple beauty."

"Yes, I ... I know."

Victoria took her time pouring the wine in silence. She was still seated at the piano. She turned to face Pauly, and he met her gaze. It was a quiet, simple moment, an imperial moment nonetheless.

"Here, Pauly, come and check out what I've selected for the morning," she said, holding out a glass of wine for him. She slid over to one side of the piano bench. "Here," she said, patting the part of the piano bench she'd just slid from, "I've warmed it up for you." She did not look away from the printed sheet music in front of her.

Pauly took his wineglass and sat next to her on the piano bench. The bench was so small their bodies had to touch. Victoria wore a light and freshly starched sundress. Her skin was naturally sun-soaked from the day. She exuded a temperate heat, with wafts of sweet and ordinary perspiration. She smelled like a wildflower. She smelled alive.

They began by going through the Sunday morning music. They played a reasonable and seasoned charade. They could most certainly conduct morning mass without these intimate Saturday evening meetings.

Pauly was overwhelmingly taken with this picture and presence of beauty. His entire being felt he was being presented an injustice. The splendor and purity of this woman was too much to resist. He knew it was wrong to pursue a married woman. Yet why this woman? Why did God have to bring this woman into his life? Why did God allow such a flower to flourish right before him? Was such a flower meant to remain unattended?

Something happened. A shift in the temperament of the room occurred. Victoria was shuffling through her music, but it was an obvious ruse. It had been a ruse from the start.

"Pauly," Victoria began, "you've done so much for me, I ... you; I want to do for you. I can help you, too. I know I can help you ..." Victoria trailed off.

The silence was restored. It was radically thick. Victoria turned to face Pauly on the bench. She put one hand on top of his. She placed her other hand on his opposite knee and leaned into him. He could feel the weight of her petite and seemingly refreshed body. Her firm, understated breasts pressed against his shoulder and arm. She kissed his cheek.

There was a glowing softness in their space. A tender and peaceful essence was shared but not explained. Simple words could not provide clarification to this realm. It started with their eye contact. Then it blossomed. The very shapes and forms of the physical world changed right before their eyes. But it was not at all that surprising. That had always been the understanding, the expectation. The curves, contours, and soft slopes of their faces changed within the eyes of the other. They softened. They became more easily understood. A deeper comprehension was gained. The switch of their souls had so been illuminated.

"Its okay, Pauly. I know. I know your struggle. I can help. You've helped me so much, Pauly. I just want to ... I just want to ... its okay ... let me ..." She brought her face to rest against his cheek. He turned to meet her. Their soft lips, through a haystack of possibilities, met one another. It was a sweet, simple kiss.

Chapter 9

"Dad? Dad? Time to get up, Dad."

Nephew is here. I hadn't realized I slept. It was some kind of flash. It was time travel. Was it just a shift in the dream? It was like a door opened. I hadn't realized a door had been closed.

I try to gather my sensibilities. It seems only a moment ago. Nephew had been watching TV. He'd just put me to bed. I just shut my eyes for a moment.

"Dad?"

"Time to get up, Dad."

Nephew helps me out of my nighttime garments, disposable and otherwise, and into some loose-fitting cotton numbers. Into the wheelchair and to the bathroom we go. Afterward, I am wheeled to the dining-room table. A simple, well-balanced breakfast awaits me: doctored oatmeal and an apple. The apple has been peeled, sectioned, and sliced.

"Here, Dad," Nephew says as he reaches to prick my finger. "Let's see if we can find some fresh real estate. Your blood sugar has been ..." His voice trails off as he concentrates on pricking my finger, gathering a blood sugar reading, and jotting down the number on a piece of notebook paper. He looks serious as he writes the blood sugar reading. "Let's get one more reading," Nephew says as he repeats the process. Nephew is tense. What is he thinking about?

Deduction opts to construct a day like all other days. It started ten years ago, after my first heart attack. Maybe it started before that.

I'd been rendered inert.
~~~ I'd been rendered faulty. ~~~
I'd been rendered disconsolate.
I'd been dejected.
</div>

I am trapped by my sick and failing body. I always knew this as my fate. Somehow I am comforted by this sinking hole of depression. I know this home of misery has always been waiting for me. I feel a sense of consolation. I deserve this. I am reassured to know fate is being fulfilled.

After choking my breakfast down, Nephew wheels me to the couch, braces me to a seated position, and turns on the television.

An Exceptional Zephyr

From my picture window, the seasons have become one monotonous flow of unchanging weather. It's probably not winter. There doesn't seem to be snow on the ground, although maybe this is a brown winter. It seems doubtful. An indication of greenery, leaves, and buds is evident. It's interesting that the season has come into question. It is as though my body's finely tuned instrumentation is no longer as delicately tuned. What's the temperature of the air outside? Why can't my eyes delineate things more clearly? I suppose a mental status exam could weasel today's date out of me.

"Are you all set, Dad?"

"What?"

"I have to leave. I have to leave for just a little while this morning."

"Oh." I'm struck with a sudden sinking feeling. But I want to be alone.

"I'll only be gone for an hour or so."

"Is Junior going to come?"

"Wha? ... Ummm ... Junior? Junior probably isn't coming today. He's working."

"Did he call? Did Junior call? Why don't we call him now?"

"I have to get going, Dad. Let's try to call him later today."

"Huh, oh."

"I'll ... I'll see you. I'll see you in a little while, Dad," Nephew says hurriedly. He appears to be preoccupied with his own internal ramblings.

Nephew leaves. From the picture window I can see him make his way along the front walk. He opens the front gate and closes it behind him. He walks away. He's gone. He's been swallowed by the mass and jumble of urban concrete.

The house is stone quiet. The television babbles quietly at what seems a great distance. Its digital picture display seems artificially phosphorescent. I feel foggy. I feel far away.

The phone begins to ring. It jangles sharply through the quiet space of my house. The intervals of space between rings are heavy with weighted, vibrant silence. It seems the dust floating in the air stops and shakes with the jingle and clatter of the phone. The dust goes on drifting in the paused silence.

I am unable to move independently. The phone is out of reach. I have to let it ring. Eventually, after the allotted five rings, my voice comes up on the answering message. As my voice greets the caller, I hope they decide to leave a message. The caller begins while the answering machine records the memorandum.

"Hey, Dad ... Nephew, how are you guys doing? It's Junior. I just wanted to call and let you know I made it home

An Exceptional Zephyr 〜 65

and ... I meant to call last night ... but ... well hey, I really hope you are doing well. Give me a call, or I will give you a call. Well all right. Um, talk to you guys soon."

I begin to cry. Junior is so close. His voice is ... it's my little boy. The deepest and most veiled chords within are so easily made to reverberate simply by the reproduction of his voice over the recording.

He hangs up. Junior hangs up. The blanket of silence again settles over the house. Such profound layers. My mind is abuzz with the electricity of swirling thoughts and possibilities. My soul is alive with gratitude and bottomless longing.

Something isn't feeling right. I feel dreamily disconnected, much more than usual. I feel heavy and foggy. Are my emotions burdened by Junior's voice message? Why am I suddenly feeling so dreadfully, yet peacefully, out of place? Am I beginning to feel better? Is this grave and weighted feeling getting worse? I don't think this is pain. Is there pain? Did Nephew give me the proper dosage of insulin with my breakfast?

I try to concentrate on the television. The picture is wonderfully animated. Has it always been this luminescent? The sound isn't right. Is the volume too low? It sounds like it's coming through water. My eyes are blurry. I don't think it should be this difficult to keep them open. Maybe I need a nap? Should I close my eyes? Maybe I'll close my eyes for just a wink.

I pop my eyes open in a panic. What is happening to me? Something is wrong. I try to move. Shifting my body is much more difficult than usual. I wonder how much time has passed. When will Nephew return? Am I overreacting? I feel frightfully faint. Am I breathing properly?

I think to activate the emergency push button on my wristband. Maybe I'll give it another series of moments. Maybe my breakfast is just settling. Maybe I need to poopy. My breath feels short. I'll just rest. I'll just rest my eyes.

Chapter 10

I suddenly feel delightfully light. I realize I am without problems, physical or otherwise. I recognize I am without a body. The realization strikes me as the more familiar. This is more known than if I were with my body. I'm floating near the ceiling of my living room. Then I float to a place of great knowledge and awareness, although it's not a place I could describe very well. I seem to wisp and twirl with complete freedom, like an untethered ribbon.

It's still. It's filled with so much. Everything. The stillness has a sound, but I can't tell what it is. I can see ... I can see how bright it is. It's white and shiny. It's a hospital room. The room is abuzz. Rose is here. She's lying as though in an adult-sized car seat. Her body is prone. Her legs are spread. She is affixed by her ankles. The apparatus is made of stainless steel. She is in an upright position. She lies at waist level. A doctor is between her legs. There seems to be a tense yet content satisfaction in the room. Junior is being born ... my little baby boy. It's all so dramatic, exciting, and simple, and assorted with joy. I can see the crown of Junior's head popping out. Now he's all the way out. He came out from inside Rose. Rose and I hold him simultaneously. We all smile and cry. Everything is so wonderful. There are so many things. Everything is so easy. I understand. I understand now ...

I float again. I float away. I float to somewhere.

I can see the dirt road in front of my village home in South America. How strange. The sun is so warm on my skin. It's so specific. Its bright, warmish, yellow light is so very close. I feel so connected. The smells are ... Is this a dream? This is a dream, of that I am certain. I can smell kerosene. I can smell the nearby presence of cows and sheep. How wonderful this all is. How ethereal and delicate. The shadow has been lifted. Everything sparkles with such warm, soft light.

In the frosty light of the dirt road and the surrounding village, a mother and child approach. It's Rose and Junior; they walk hand in hand. Rose and Junior are home with me in South America.

There is a schoolyard near where I stand. The lawn of the schoolyard is so brightly green. The grounds are very well used and tended. They remain scrubby. Children's frolics can be seen and heard. Families are here. It is recess. Everyone is happy and free.

The sun is so perfect. Its warmth and light are entirely and perfectly from heaven.

Rose and Junior continue to approach me up the dusty dirt road. Simple village homes line the single-lane, dirt car path. I begin to walk toward them. I begin to walk toward Rose and Junior. We close the gap. I feel such light elation. Their specifics are not yet fully discernible. But the mood is right. The mood is immaculate. I can sense peace. I am peace. It is the connection to a sense of tranquility and simple delight. I am that connection. They are smiling. I am smiling, too. We just walk toward each other. There seems to be such gladness in this simple transitory movement.

As the gap between us closes, it becomes a great deal brighter. This vision is fading. This vision is fading into the bright light. A sudden darkness encompasses us. The specificity of these bright happenings is being torn away. It seems a sharp slap has messed up everything. A dreadful jolt has smeared this wonderful scene.

I am pulled through a murky shadow by a force I am unable to identify. Glimmers of a small town are outside. This is the town to which Rose and I moved immediately following our marriage. This is the small town of Luck. The surroundings are horribly dark. It's not just dark, it's void of color. It's gray, murky, and shadowed. It's cold. The most gray, the most alone. I had not yet known a void like this.

I am slapped again. This time into blackness.

I think someone is slapping me.

"Rahja!"

"Rahja!"

Someone is shouting my name. Are the sounds coming through a tunnel? I can feel a piercing sensation in my ears. The sound is such that it warbles my ears, rolls my eyes, and makes me dizzy. I am lying down. I can feel a sense of bodily inertia, although I am affixed. I open my eyes, mainly in an effort to verify it is possible. I feel blinded. It's hazy and bright. A young gentleman clothed in emergency attire is directly in front of me. A woman, dressed for an emergency, sits nearby. They look serious and bored. I am in an ambulance. We're racing somewhere. It seems as though we are in quite a hurry.

I begin to float again. I can see the ambulance from above. I seem to keep rising as the ambulance races on. I can see the paramedics. They're frantic. I am suddenly very peaceful. I don't share their sense of panic.

Another bout of blackness ... this one isn't ... what is this? How can I explain? The only words or description I can conjure up has to do with a sharp yet soft beam of light that makes up my entire horizon. It's somehow everywhere. It's present in all directions. It's limitless. It's endless. It's bigger than the sky. It washes and cascades into deeper shades of gray as it moves away from its white-lit circular center. The beam of perfectly white light is in the middle. Shades of graying darkness move off in directions on the top and bottom from my perspective of it. I float like a red ribbon somewhere within this infinite expanse. I know it's peaceful here, but I'm not entirely at ease.

Chapter 11

The affair continued. It gained a better degree of traction once the charade ended. It was then that the real farce could begin. It went on for years. It never really ended, although it did hit hard times on several occasions.

In many ways, the church rectory served as an ideal refuge. It was a place Padre Pauly could find solace and retreat from the demands of a public parish. It also served as a cove of seclusion for him and Victoria. Conversely, it was the place in which people knew he could be found. In certain respects, it was good for hiding. However, everyone was familiar with the hideout.

On one occasion, Stanley came. The rectory was such that most parishioners just walked in. That's what Stanley did. Once in the lobby, however, he paused. He wondered. A bit of the fire and confusion he'd felt on the walk over was fading. He was in the home of a servant, a servant of the Lord Father.

Pauly also wondered. He sat behind the desk in his study. The large heavy desk stood before a window that overlooked a better part of Morningstar. Off in the distance, behind the town, sat a lake. The lake was still. The day was overcast and calm. The air was humid with precipitation, but none yet fell. Padre Pauly had watched Stanley approach the rectory. He heard Stanley enter. He could feel Stanley's presence in the lobby. Both men were silent. Both men detected the presence of the other.

Quietly, Padre Pauly stood. He made his way out of the office and down the stairs. "Hello, Stanley," Pauly said, extending his hand. He wore a warm relaxed smile.

"Hi, Padre," Stanley said, extending his hand as well. He looked mentally tired. He was not freshly shaven. He smelled of Old English cologne, sleep, and stale beer.

The two men were caught in the overthrows of silence. Volumes of unsaid discourse trailed in each of their heads.

"Would you like something to drink?" Padre Pauly asked, breaking the awkward silence.

"Yeah, that would be good."

An Exceptional Zephyr   75

The two men retired to the parlor. They sat in old leather chairs, which were positioned in front of an extinguished fireplace. The season hadn't yet called for a fire. However, it was clear small fires had recently been built. Pauly looked to the fireplace and thought of Victoria. Stanley looked to the fireplace and wondered through the best of his intentions, despite this blatant indication. The men sat. They took sips from glass tumblers of whiskey.

Pauly took the lead and exercised the experience of his adulated role. He thought it may be advantageous. He thought to begin and align their talk properly. It may grow to be an awkward exchange. "Stanley, how may I be of service today?"

Stanley took his time. It was difficult for Pauly to discern whether Stanley was upset. He wore an absentminded expression. "Padre, what I am about to say, I say with the utmost respect and reverence for you and the Church. I … I am not here to question or accuse. I, but I, I have a strong sense of. I, well, of course it's no secret, you and Victoria seem to spend a helluva lot of time together. I, I know some … some around town have been sayin' it don't seem right. Well, I don't think it's anyone's gotdamn bit of business either way. I guess …"

Stanley paused. Pauly thought about jumping in but then thought otherwise. Stanley continued.

"Pauly, I trust you. And I trust the house of the Lord. I don't know all about the business of the Lord. But I do know you been doin' a fine job. My wife, well Victoria, she's devout, as you well know I'm sure. I'm not here to question you, Padre. Some of the people in town been talkin'. Got me fired up at first. But I realize ... I realize after I thought about it, I trust the house of the Lord and, you know what, Pauly, I'm grateful ya give my wife such a nice spot. She's devout, Pauly. Well I don't need to tell you that. And, well, she loves to be given a purpose and, well, I ... I guess that is what I came here to say. I ... I thank ya, Padre."

Pauly let the moment breathe. Something in him wanted to speak immediately to fill the air. But another part of him wanted to speak in order to fervently agree and praise Stanley's line of thinking. He didn't. He allowed himself to be quiet.

After a while, he spoke. "I thank you, Stanley. Judge not lest be judged ... and ..." Pauly couldn't go on. He knew what he was doing with Victoria was wrong. And here, instead of being punished like he had expected, he was being praised. He was being praised by Victoria's husband. Quite suddenly, he didn't know what to say.

Chapter 12

I'm awake. I am propped up and bedded with plush and fluffy pillows. Yet I am far from comfortable. My whole body feels tormented. The surroundings are white, unnaturally soft, and sterile. Tubes and medical appliances inundate the small space. My wiener is fastened and pinched by a catheter. I am in a hospital room again. How long will this go on? I am too weak and medicated to speak. These trips to the hospital ... they're a dark convention; they've become my dark tendency.

Nephew is at my side. He has such a serious look. Where is Junior? There is so much to say. There is so much to do. It doesn't matter. I'm frantic. I'm not sure why. I feel a sense of impending or unresolved energy. I know this extent of confused and seemingly contradictory emotions are ultimately from a place of happiness. Yes, that's it! But why all these tears? Why this unstoppable river of catharsis?

"Time to rest now, Dad," Nephew says with parental deportment. "Let those tears get some sleep, Dad. You need rest, Dad. Shhh," Nephew says, putting his pointer finger over his puckered lips.

I cry myself into a deep, dreamless, and pharmaceutically induced sleep.

───※───

I awake to Junior and Nephew at my bedside. I break into an uncontrolled fit of crying. I am very emotional. Nephew, Junior, and the duty nurse try to placate me. I don't think they understand my emotion and grief. I don't know if I understand the flood or barrage of tears. I don't know if words can explain.

Tears of disconnection
~~~   Tears of happiness.   ~~~

I obsess about the vision I had in the ambulance. Was it the hereafter? It stuck to the very center of my bones. Perhaps it had something to do with the immense generation of tears. I feel less a part of this world. That beam of light: it wasn't a tunnel. It was a beaming, white sunset. It was a horizon that went on forever, an endless sphere of soft, brilliant, white light. I just floated in its limitless span. I knew nothing was there. Yet I knew it was the genesis of all things. Was it God? It didn't seem like others were its presence. Yet, I didn't feel to be entirely alone. I don't know. I am wordless to capture its drifting and all-encompassing essence.

Others come to see me in the hospital. I just cry. I keep on weeping. I don't know what to do. I guess I need the purging. I hope they understand. I can feel their embarrassment. I don't think they know what to do.

An insulin imbalance was the culprit for me being sent to the hospital. Other factors were also at play. My congenital heart failure, supranuclear palsy, and inconsistent kidney function seem to keep the doctors challenged with how to reliably treat me. Apparently the heart remains crucial to the function of everything else.

I am released from the hospital's intensive care unit after about a week. I am sent to a nursing home. It isn't permanent; it's a rehabilitation facility. I am to be evaluated to determine whether I can return home. I've been through this rigmarole on more than a few occasions. The rehabilitation staff is wonderfully encouraging. They're also dreadfully uncompromising. They smile through my sweat. I just want to go home.

After nearly a month of evaluations and reevaluations, I am comfortably returned to my couch. This is good. I have much to think about.

"Dad," Nephew says. "Dad," he says again. "Time to do your exercises, Dad," Nephew pleasantly persists.

Nephew hands me what appears to be a large rubber band. Or maybe it more closely resembles a chintzy, plastic, waistband. It's ridiculous. I am supposed to perform simple stretching exercises with this rehabilitation device.

"C'mon, Dad, over your head," Nephew encourages.

I am pretty stubborn about the whole thing. It's humiliating. I can't get past the childlike insinuation of it all. At my age, someone should be doing the exercises for me. I've been through this already. Maybe I'm missing the point of it all. Is there a point?

"C'mon, Dad, with your legs now. Put it over the bottom of your foot. Here, like this." Nephew demonstrates with effortless agility.

My right leg doesn't work too well anymore. They took veins out of my leg for one of my bypass surgeries. That's when my leg quit working properly. It's as if the messages don't go all the way down my leg anymore. Then they thought the nerves in my neck were pinched. In that instance, they performed a surgical procedure to create more space in the duct of my vertebra. Maybe my leg worked for a while. I don't remember.

"All right, Dad. That's good. Good work, Dad."

I wonder if Nephew understands the fruitlessness of all this? He seems to honor me as an elder. He seems to honor the idea of caring for me as his elder. But what is he supposed to do, tell me not to do my exercises? He's under all sorts of allegations anyway. What must others think? Nephew has a wife and two children back in South America. He is thousands of miles from his home. His temporary travel visa has long since expired, and he's no longer here legally. What must Junior think? But would Junior honor this custom—this custom of caring for me in my home? I wasn't around for all those years ... more than ten years. Junior and I were estranged for more than ten years ... no contact. The sense of anguish from those lost years is always right around the corner. The anguish is ready. The anguish is always ready to sneak up on me. The anguish is merciless.

Nephew props me up on the couch and leaves the room.

It's good to be home. This time is different, though. I've made the tour several times now—into the ambulance, to the hospital, to a nursing home, and back to my couch.

I am much quieter. Nephew has begun to engage me with thoughtful concern. He can sense a change. He doesn't understand my reticence. Do I understand it? I think I do. I think he does, too.

I begin to think about less, yet my mind is more openly clear. I am immeasurably fuller, yet I am more disconnected to this physical world. I am leaving this world. I have a much clearer idea and understanding of what that means. Yet how to explain?

I drift off to sleep.

Chapter 13

The eternal expanse of the everlasting appears again. I am closer this time. It's wholly peaceful. Words do little service to the range and experience of my consciousness.

There is less fading to the darkness on the upper and lower portions. I just seem to float here. I am merely intertwined as a drifting thread in the ever-changing fabric of silence. I don't have a body. It occurs to me that perhaps I could fall. Then I begin moving in a direction both toward the beaming white sunset and also slightly downward. I have the sensation of intense speed. The orientation of the frosty, white-lit horizon doesn't seem to really change much.

Then I'm with Rose and Junior. Junior is in a stroller. We walk along a perfect little street in the small town of Luck. It's a perfect summer evening. I am aware of everything—the shade of the evening sky and the smells. I am inundated. This is the woman with whom I've created this beautiful child. The smell of a peachy baby hangs in the air. I can also smell the tart zest of a freshly made rhubarb pie. We just walk. We amble past Lucky's Barbershop. The spinning marquee is always so unintentionally curious. Junior always points and laughs from his stroller. It seems to mark a signpost. But is it more than that?

This is my heaven, these walks in Luck. The dream progresses into a collage of small-town walks. Following our marriage, we moved to Luck, Minnesota. That's where we started our life together. We struggled. However, these walks could solve anything. These walks became our assenting slice of heaven. We always knew it. But how can I thoughtfully express it?

I am flung from the dreamy experience. I seem to pass a flash, or there is an awareness of the eternal, beaming, white sunset.

I am back on my couch. Nephew is standing over me. It is dark outside. The TV is off. It appears to be late. A certain quiet has descended. Nephew is attired in his sleeping apparel.

"Time for bed, Dad. Dad?"

"Yes."

"Are you okay, Dad? You slept like a log all day. You didn't move. ... I ... I um ..."

"Yes, I'm okay."

Nephew sits with me for a moment. He seems to be captivated, lost in his thoughts. Then he quietly helps me into my wheelchair. He wheels me to my bed in the dining room. As he undresses me, he makes a soiling discovery.

"Ayyee Dad, I think ya pooped yourself, Dad."

I had no idea.

I am soon washed and lying in bed. The house is dark and quiet. The outside noises of a busy city can be heard, but they seem far away.

I am wide-awake. There is so much to think about. The dream I just had is losing its specific intensity, but the remnants are still a flicker.

I think about my time with Rose in Luck. We'd gone away to become a family. And we did. We were a family. Our lives were so delightfully quaint. It had been so perfect. It had been so simple, hadn't it?

But what happened. Why was it ... why did it go away?

A dark and ominous shadow becomes known as I ruminate in thought.

I drank.
~~~ I drank my family away. ~~~
I drank my family gone.

</div>

In only four years. In four years, we were back to Revelation Falls. We'd exhausted everything. The drink wore us out. Rose left me. I'd never considered that within the realm of any possibility.

Rose filed for divorce. We'd only been married for four years. Those were ugly times, dark times. Those were the times that helped me understand the root of gloom and obscurity.

I saw Junior until he was six years old.

<div style="text-align:center">

The drinking hid the darkness.
~~~ The drinking shadowed the darkness. ~~~
The shadow was in the drink.
The drinking held me in the dark.

It became too complicated to see Junior. I was hurt. I was hurt to the core of my bones. I don't think my heart was able or willing to understand. In fact, there wasn't anything to understand. Such things aren't meant to be understood. The cavity of such emotional torment is ... it's a wonder any human can even imagine, let alone experience. So began the years.

<p style="text-align:center">It was time to get serious.
~~~   I began a more diligent allegiance.   ~~~
I could fully commit myself now,
The drink and I.</p>

Chapter 14

Rose was a conscientious and well-intentioned single mother to Junior. While she struggled on many levels, she was determined to provide a stable, secure, and enriched home. That included the makings of a traditional family Christmas for the two of them.

Through a slightly frosted window, Rose watched Junior play in the snow. Earlier he'd been playing with some of the other neighborhood kids. Now he was playing alone. Rose surmised the neighbor kids had been called home to begin with their Christmas Eve revels and traditions. She watched him play. She watched Junior with intention. Seeing him all alone awakened her own feelings of sadness. She couldn't quite reach what it was. Seeing her little boy all alone, playing next to the neighborhood swing set, awakened in her a sense of loneliness. Watching her little Junior made for unfulfilled feelings of yearning and connection. She thought of Rahja, and all at once felt a pang of bewilderment and a strange sense of relief. She was confused for her wanting of a relationship yet basked in the space of solitude. Watching little Junior brought further feelings of respite and autonomy. Something about his youth and childhood vigor made for open feelings and the ever-present stir of possibilities. She called to him, "Junior, honey, Junior, come in now. C'mon honey."

Junior paused. It was as though he didn't want to be interrupted. Yet he too was somehow, in some deep way, enthralled by the potential unfolding of optimistic opportunity.

"C'mon, honey," Rose continued. "We'll open our gifts from Santa."

At this, Junior made for a more hasty and concerted effort toward their low-income housing unit.

Once inside the kitchen entrance door, Junior shook off the cold and snow. He doffed his little Sorel snow boots and his snowmobile suit. Rose stowed the boots on a secondhand macramé rug. She hung the suspendered snowmobile suit on a coat hook. She could smell the ozone and outside cold coming off her little boy. Junior could smell freshly made bread and the seasoning of Minnesota hot dish. Rose and Junior were both unknowingly warmed by the presence of each other.

Rose watched as Junior proceeded to the adjoining living room. He examined the unlit Christmas tree and all the wrapped gifts underneath. It struck Rose as odd that she had not yet plugged in the Christmas tree lights. All the other Christmas decorations were lit.

A wave of late day blues struck Rose again. The day was still lit, but the sun had been swallowed by the horizon. She looked at her little boy with a sense of sorrow she didn't understand. It seemed provoked by the unlit Christmas tree.

Meanwhile, Junior excitedly examined the horde of wrapped gifts. He was tickled with excitement. A pile of Lego's was still out from an earlier session of play. He didn't know if he should resume his Lego building operation or begin pleading with his mother to open gifts. Junior was already beginning to sense the idea that sometimes anticipation is better than the tangible moment of grasp.

Rose joined Junior in the living room. She tickled his neck and ruffled his hair. He laughed and shrugged his shoulders in a movement of both evasion and play. "Junior, honey, why don't we open one gift now, before dinner? Then we'll eat and open the rest after dinner. How does that sound, honey?"

"Yeah, Mom, yeah. Let's do that."

"But first, let me plug in these Christmas tree lights. How could I have forgotten?"

Junior sat across the room, examining the Christmas tree and all the gifts underneath. He began an earnest effort of trying to determine which one to open first. There were many to choose from. As he looked at the gifts, he watched his mother.

Rose bent to her hands and knees and crawled clumsily behind the Christmas tree. She secured the strung Christmas tree lights plug but then paused momentarily. She was apprehensive for a moment. Then she shrugged and married the plug with the electrical wall socket. At the moment the plug engaged the wall socket, a flash of light and a loud pop startled the room. They both jumped in surprise. Their attention was all at once sharply focused by adrenaline. Junior remained seated, watching his mother turn quickly. She shakily and abruptly turned from the electrical socket. She remained on her hands and knees by the Christmas tree. She bent away, trying to create distance from both the tree and the wall socket. She looked to Junior. Her face was flatly blackened. The black gave a chalky appearance. Junior laughed. He couldn't contain himself. It was reminiscent of any one of several cartoons he'd seen where an electrical shock blackened the cartoon character's face.

"Junior, don't laugh. This isn't funny." Thankfully, Rose was fine. She had been startled and frustrated, but the sudden surge of electricity did her no harm. As she later explained, a very tiny thread of wire was popping out of the electrical socket before she'd plugged in the Christmas tree lights. The electrician explained that was what had likely caused the surge and electrical short.

For the moment, Junior just went on laughing. He just couldn't help himself.

Chapter 15

Nephew was lost down the back alleyways of his own reverie.

It was just before noon. The sun was near its hottest. Most of his village neighbors were beginning their late morning siestas. Wrought-knotted hammocks were the most popular manner of catching midday winks. Virtually all South American villagers possessed at least one hammock per household. The work ethic was such that little expectation was given to whether villagers returned to work in the afternoon. Unless you were a business owner or had some other vested interest in a paid occupation, you may or may not work consistently. That's just the way it was.

Nephew sat. While others of the village neighborhood nestled into some shady spot for an hour or two of shut-eye, Nephew remained wide-awake. His thoughts and energies were tangled and keyed up. He'd just received another letter from the United States of America, a letter from his uncle Rahja. This was a letter of invitation. This was a letter of confirmation. These were what dreams were made of. Villagers of this northeastern rainforest community could only wish for such an opportunity. His uncle Rahja had been one of very few who had successfully immigrated to the land of opportunity, the land of milk and honey, the land where wishes and riches were simply how people lived. How could this be? This was so wonderful.

Nephew's wife came to where he sat. She stood behind him and laid a hand on his shoulder. Together they shared amped and laden silence.

They owned a small house together in the rainforest community on the northeastern coast of South America. Here they resided with their two young children. They did relatively well by comparison with others, but their portion of South America was dreadfully poor. The country had nothing to speak of in the way of resources. Medical care, government infrastructure, and human welfare, not to mention employment opportunities, were mostly unheard of. Blatant corruption among government officials was the expectation. While the villagers did well in caring for themselves and one another, it was a difficult existence.

Nephew and his wife sat in serious silence. They looked across the expanse of their rough rainforest yard. Large exotic plants busied the landscape. Speckles of bright hot sunlight broke through the tropical rooftop. The air was thick and nourishing with fresh precipitation. The vegetation was unkempt and beautiful. The forest floor was nearly black and spongy. A small group of wild parrots flew by and landed on a distant tree. A small lizard scurried up the trunk of a young mango tree. Other furry creatures milled about unseen. Nephew likely didn't realize the oasis he was preparing to depart. This was the only life he or his family knew.

So much remained unknown or unanswered. Nephew would be leaving everything he knew. He would be leaving everyone he knew. His uncle Rahja's invitations had become more insistent. While he knew his uncle had taken ill, he didn't know to what extent. Yet his mind was swirling on other matters. He thought of securing his citizenship of the United States of America. It surely wouldn't take too long to become a fully bona fide citizen of the United States, He thought of eventually bringing his wife and his children to the United States. How difficult could it possibly be? He thought of wearing finely tailored garments. He thought of bustling skyscrapers. He thought of finely tuned, luxury motor vehicles. He thought of the mansion his uncle Rahja must live in. Did his uncle have servants? He couldn't believe it. He felt like he was in a dream.

Nephew's wife nuzzled his neck. "Ooo," she said, "you're going to need a haircut before you leave. Let's take you to the village market and have it done right, a shave with the hot water and the towel, and everything. I heard the market barber just got a new sign. Apparently it's mechanical and spins. I didn't understand, but everyone has been talking all about it. Apparently there is something quite magical about it. Let's go get you a haircut, honey."

Chapter 16

I quit drinking more than ten years ago. I could have probably quit years earlier. I could have probably quit while I was still married to Rose. Padre Pauly tried to help me. He tried to help me quit drinking. I'd seen him on the brief occasion that I visited Rose in her family home. I always thought it strange that a retired Catholic priest lived with Rose's mother, Victoria. Pauly and I entertained an occasional outing from time to time. I don't know what it was about him. I took a very companionable and surrendered liking to him. I think he thought of me as a son. He had a unique way of talking with me. He was an immensely hearty man. He was a salty German from a small town in northern Minnesota, near the Canadian border. He was strong and weathered from the many changed seasons and frigid winters. Yet he had such a soft character. He had such a quiet wisdom. I don't know what propelled him into priesthood. I only knew him after he retired. His living arrangements with Victoria baffled me, but I gave it little thought. I also came to know Rose's father, Stanley. He and Victoria had divorced some years before I came to know Rose. Rose helped make some sense of the strange tangle of associations.

As I remember, Rose said,

> Oh, yes, Padre Pauly ran a small church in a little northern town, way up north near the Canadian border. That's where my mom met him. I was about nine years old when she and Padre Pauly met. That was in Morningstar. That was our hometown. She chased Pauly relentlessly. I don't know why she felt so irresistibly drawn to him. My dad took a pretty lax role in our family. He worked at the local bar. I guess if he wasn't actually working, he was there drinking. It was the only bar in town. My dad was an enormously gentle man. He just wasn't around. He probably had a drinking problem.
>
> I think Padre Pauly sort of looked after us. My younger sisters hadn't yet been born. I know my mom pleaded with Padre Pauly to leave the Church and marry her. I remember sneaking around with her at strange hours. We'd go to the church or the rectory. All of us kids were often left in the lobby or in one of

the sitting rooms, while my mom and Padre Pauly were off doing who knows what.

It created quite the little controversy in Morningstar. So much so that Padre Pauly was repeatedly reprimanded by the Church. It was ... you know how small towns are. Everybody knows something about everyone else. Padre Pauly was eventually forced to move to a parish in another town. My mom moved the family. Can you believe it? She moved all of us. Can you imagine? We followed Padre Pauly. My dad, he just stayed in Morningstar. It was a strange childhood.

Eventually my mom and dad divorced. My dad just stayed in that small town. He just stayed working at the bar. He didn't do much for us kids. We ended up moving to the closest city, Revelation Falls. The state university was there. After a time, Padre Pauly was spending more time around our house in Revelation Falls. I don't know. Eventually he just moved in. I guess it didn't feel especially weird.

My mom became pregnant during the time of her divorce from my dad. There is some speculation as to whether the baby belonged to my dad or Padre Pauly. Can you imagine? He was a Catholic priest after all.

I always thought the story was almost entirely twisted. It didn't seem to be in Padre Pauly's character. He must have known how ferocious the path of drinking could be. He was trying to help me figure it out. I knew it was bad.

But the thought of the sweet drink still soothes me, somehow, after all these years.

I'd like to think the time Rose and I spent in Luck, Minnesota, was good. But I know it wasn't.

Chapter 17

On one very surprising occasion, the bishop of the diocese paid Padre Pauly an unannounced visit.

It was a rainy day. The cold rain fell steadily. As evening drew near, it was likely the rain would turn to sleet or snow. That type of weather, that time of the year, was every bit as common as an abundant crop. It was just a normal sleepy evening. The days were shorter and the nights longer as winter made its approach. Little Morningstar had begun to hunker down.

Padre Pauly had built a fire in the hearth. Victoria was in the rectory kitchen, preparing a simple meal from the season's harvest. They maintained a good degree of discretion in their secret relationship. Nevertheless, it began to feel as though any sort of threat to their association was of little relevance. Stanley, Victoria's husband, had essentially dismissed his concerns to the trust of Pauly and the

Church. People of the town certainly voiced their opinions of the matter to one another. They held sharp viewpoints. But estimations or profanations of talk did little to affect any real change. In some ways, the scandalous rumors over such tantalizing matters only fueled the affair and acted as its own distraction. The tales sailed on the wisps of the wind, as rumors often do, gathering prickly but inconsistent attention.

Fresh wood popped in the fireplace as the warm and restorative fire grew on its own. A palette of rich and sophisticated smells radiated from the kitchen. Rain pitter-pattered on the roof as a steady force. The season's harvest had been reaped. Much of the year's work had come to a close. Lazy attitudes pervaded the homes and people of Morningstar. A renewed sense of peace and leisure settled over the town like a balmy bedspread.

"Dinner's ready, Pauly. Would you like to eat in the dining room, or shall we eat by the fire. I think we ought to eat in front of—"

A sturdy knock at the door interrupted Victoria's inquiry. Pauly and Victoria looked at each other with a light sense of surprise. While it was strange that someone should knock at the door, little if any threat was felt. Should it? Who could Saturday evening possibly be bringing to the door?

As both Pauly and Victoria approached the door, it opened. In preparation for dinner, Pauly had begun to extinguish his tobacco pipe. Victoria held a plate of steaming food for each of them.

Standing in the doorway, shaking off the rain, was the bishop of the diocese. It was surreal to both Victoria and Padre Pauly. A pillar of leadership and reverence was in their very midst. The bishop resided over one hundred miles to the south. Pauly and Victoria were primarily shocked. Nonetheless, the practice of their affair had better prepared them for such unanticipated events. The engagement of their affair was wrong. The experiences in maintaining their indiscretions naturally groomed them for the unexpected.

"Well, good evening, Bishop. To what do we owe this lovely surprise?" Padre Pauly faltered and tried to gain his footing. The bishop continued to shake off the rain and cold. As he did, he looked up and surveyed the room. He eyed Pauly and Victoria with a keen but gentle eye. In those few moments of silence, Pauly wished he hadn't addressed the bishop using the word "we."

"Well, good evening, Pauly. And well, good evening to you, my dear." The bishop, too, although knowingly prepared, was caught off guard.

"We, or ..." Pauly began.

"That's okay. Pauly, let's grab just a moment. It's been a long drive. I, do you have a bit of something to sip? Something to warm me from the inside out?"

"Yes, yes. Let us sit in the parlor."

"Bishop, Father Pauly, can I get you anything while I'm here?" Victoria asked. She thought to assume and display a subservient role. She thought it might cover what probably didn't appear to be a very appropriate evening between herself and Padre Pauly.

"No, no thank you," said the bishop, paying little attention.

"Thank you, Victoria. That will be all." Pauly felt strange addressing Victoria that way. He felt stuck. He would likely face a later scolding from Victoria. Nevertheless, he had to consider the magnitude of what could currently be happening between he and the bishop.

Pauly and the bishop climbed the stairs to the second-floor landing and entered the parlor. They sat adjacent to each other on the sofa and leather chair. Pauly poured them each a small tipple of whiskey. No ice was offered. Pauly could hear the entrance door open and close as Victoria took leave. Pauly's heart sank. So much seemed suddenly unknown, so out of control. How had all become so quickly lost?

"Let me get right to it, Pauly. It's pretty well clear what is going on here."

"Bishop, I—" Pauly tried to interject.

"No, Pauly," the bishop said, holding up a hand. "Let me make clear as to why I am here and how we do this."

Pauly let out a breath. A current of optimism ran through him. It was difficult to know why. Part of him thought that perhaps what the bishop had to say wasn't so bad. Another part of him knew he could maintain his affair with Victoria regardless of what was said.

"Pauly, this thing with this woman has got to end. We've received a number of complaints and inquiries. It's certainly not uncommon and of little consequence—provided you nip this thing in the bud right now. It sounds like the woman just left. Unfortunate, as we could have provided her a bit of, well, collaborative counsel. Nevertheless, I trust you'll do what you need to. These sorts of things pass anyway. Thank the Lord we're not talking about someone of the male persuasion. Or, Jesus, an altar boy. That would be a much different scenario. These things, for a young man like you, they happen sometimes. Pauly, let's make sure we do the right thing. So you got off track. Now it's time to ... well, you know."

Pauly invited the bishop to stay, hoping he wouldn't. The bishop explained, "Nah, Padre. I've got a driver this evening, who is still waiting in the car. I'll grab a quick bite. It smells like that woman is quite the cook."

Pauly and the bishop ate mostly in silence. It appeared as though the bishop felt his job had fundamentally been delivered. Pauly pondered the difficulty he might encounter making peace with Victoria. He hoped she wasn't upset. He also wondered about leaving. He'd likely always stay with the Church, but could he leave Morningstar? Could he be transferred to another parish?

Chapter 18

I drift to a sleepy state of unsettled visions and memories of episodes in Luck. The dreamscape is a blurry mix of shadowed nightmare and some kind of charming simplicity. Any sense of dichotomy fuses to a single spectrum.

The sweet and sinister syrup of brandy had me within its engaging and charismatic grip. I'd been at the Polished Piranha Tavern. The Piranha was just below our small-town apartment in Luck. The visions are blurry and disconnected. The soft, yellow, illumination of old lightbulbs; the aged, ratty wood; the encompassing blanket of lavender cigarette and cigar smoke; and the recognition of familiar barroom faces, most of whom were as drunk as I. The dysfunctional den was homey. I loved spending my time at the Piranha.

I was in a rage one particular evening. I forget the specifics of why I was so wildly angry. I see myself knocking over a table. A smattering of glass hit the carpeted floor with a clatter. I was fuming. I was fuming like a bull. I was consumed with revenge and a primitive sense of justice. I dashed from the Piranha through the outdoor corridor and up the stairs to our second-floor apartment. I flew through the door. Rose was watching a television program. She was serene yet anticipating my arrival home. Our plain and uncomplicated abode was void of many possessions. It was very clean, smelling of fresh linen, diluted Pine-Sol, and bleach. A single pink candle burned in the windowsill. My rage failed to see the delight and simplicity of this tranquility. This was my home, our home. Rose was up waiting for me. Junior was peacefully asleep in the next room.

I'd often departed in the evening on the guise that I was only leaving for a pack of cigarettes. I'd lie. Instead of returning home, I'd go to the bar. On this occasion, in my rage, I grabbed a knife and stormed from the apartment. Rose tried to stop me. She just wanted to understand what could be going on. In my frenzied state, I pushed her aside. She wanted so badly to gather even a fraction of appreciation or acknowledgment. She wanted to be a part of my world. She wanted our lives to coalesce. The ease and plainness of her desires were always so endearing. However, I never saw it that way. I was more interested in being a man.

I stormed from the apartment. I had to return to the Piranha Tavern with the knife. Justice required maintenance. I returned to the bar, but by then, it was all different. I was presented a scene far unlike the scene of my exodus. The table I'd tipped over had been corrected. The glass had been cleaned up. Several patrons had departed. Mac, the proprietor, was waiting near the door. He was a large man. Nevertheless, his eyes were soft and sympathetic. He pacified me. He fed me a very weak brandy soda. Little did I know the beverage contained only soda pop. He fed me a small meal, too, even though the kitchen had long been closed.

My thoughts of Luck drift from the Polished Piranha. I remember inconsiderately and arrogantly knocking on the door of a neighboring apartment. The apartment housed two adorably young and cute college girls. I wondered if Rose could hear me knocking. Would Rose be angry or hurt if she could hear? I was aware of the anxiety of doing what I shouldn't. I was also aware of exercising my independence. Part of me thought avoiding such an opportunity would be unquestionably oversighted. Just then the door opened.

"Good evening," I began.

"Hi," one of the girls said shyly, with an innocent demeanor of appeal.

"Good evening and salutations," I exclaimed with fervor and comic innuendo. "Is there a prince residing with you this evening, because you are surely nothing less than a princess?" I was a bit drunk. The young girl giggled and looked at me with restless anticipation. I continued, "I am presently off to enjoy a well-earned and delightfully nourishing libation. Would you and your roommate kindly care to join me?"

"No ... I am sorry. We're ... we are ... off to study. I'm sorry," she said with a childlike smile.

The door closed. Strangely, I was relieved.

On yet another occasion, the splinters and flashes of recollection are more scattered. Visions of a particularly rambunctious night at the Polished Piranha enlighten and then go dark. The evening seemed to start with hearty laughter. A small group of us left the bar and entered a car waiting outside. The evening was frightfully cold, although by that time, we were well fueled with the sweet, liquid heat of brandy. We were driving along lonely country roads. While it was dreadfully frigid outside the swiftly moving car, the interior was nearly hot from the proximity of our bodies and the heater fan. We passed a bottle of cheap bourbon. At one point, I remember the feeling of floating weightlessness, a fit of laughter, and having to crawl from the car. Apparently we'd ended up tipped over in the ditch. In crawling out of the shattered passenger window, I knew the snow and air were cold, but I couldn't feel it.

Later that evening, after walking a distance down an old and bitterly windy country road, we ended up at someone's house. I don't know whose house it was. I remember how nice it was to feel the warmth inside. The house was stifled with cigarette smoke. A small party ensued. I lay on the floor and laughed. A couple was having sex next to me. Others in our small group laughed and carried on. At one point, I tried to get up from the floor and walk. I was unable. I laughed. I lay back down. Then my wife, Rose, and my new baby boy, Junior, settled into my mind as though a heavy, sodden wind. My laughter disappeared. I felt an enormous weight of emotional cataclysm and sorrow. I lay on the floor. I upchucked. Then I began to quietly cry in lonely isolation.

Chapter 19

"Dad ... Dad? Time to wake up, Dad." Nephew seems to encourage me with a new softness. "Dad? There are some people here to see you, Dad?"

"Yes?"

Nephew helps me out of bed. We pass through our routine of apparel exchange and elementary freshening. He helps me into my wheelchair and to the bathroom in the hallway. All the while, the small group of guests waits graciously on the couch. Because of the proximity and closeness of my first-floor living situation, they are privy to the intimacy of my basic morning routine.

Once the morning essentials are done, Nephew wheels me to the dining-room table, where my doctored oatmeal and readied apple awaits. The small group remains seated on my couch and sofa. They begin to address me.

"Good morning, Brother Rahja."

"Yes, good morning, Rahja."

"Yes," I reply. *Who are these people?* I wonder. But then I realize these are Jehovah's Witnesses. I am a Jehovah's Witness, too. It's funny. In the days when I was healthy, I wouldn't have given these people any kind of a second thought. I would have turned them away in an instant. The door would have been shut at the first hint of their conversionary aspirations. It's funny how things change. Now Jehovah's are the only ones who will still come to visit me. Nephew is here, and my dear son, sometimes. There is no one else.

I look to my guests. After looking more intently and listening to their voices, I recognize two of them. Stone begins. He is a church elder and comes to see me several times during any given week. Sometimes he drives me to the doctor. Did I mention that I don't drive? I've never really driven a car. I decided long ago to forgo the consequence of piloting a passenger vehicle. I guess it was either driving a car or partaking in the drink. The sweet and menacing drink prevailed. Nephew doesn't drive, either. He is not a citizen of the United States.

"How are you, Brother Rahja?" Stone asks.

"Fine. Yes, yes, I am doing reasonably all right."

Stone is really quite a nugget. He is so plainly wholesome. He lives with such a grounded application of goodness. He practices service. He practices humility. Stone is a family man, with two kids. He's a white man with a Korean wife. He reminds me of someone. He so easily illustrates a well-modeled example. He is a kind and generous man of God. I know he has a job. Maybe he's a teacher. I think he is a computer network instructor. He devotes an enormous amount of time to matters of Jehovah. Yet he receives no compensation for such endeavors. He must have some sort of job. Yes, I believe Stone is a computer teacher.

The other man is Mr. Bell. He is an old black man from the church. He's tall and thin. He doesn't move very quickly. He seems the type to be well versed in jive talkin'. He's peaceful and happy. He smiles frequently. He adds soft, quiet comments during his visits. He doesn't come as often as Stone, maybe a couple times in any given month. Mr. Bell makes me laugh. I'm not sure why. He gives me a very pleasant feeling. That, too, I cannot eloquently explain. In his presence, I say to myself, *Black man ... ye-es, black man.*

I don't know the third gentleman. He's young, white, and nervous looking. He wears a gray suit that looks to be a smidgen large for him. He's clean-shaven to the point that razor cuts and nicks are apparently fresh. He appears, on the whole, to be quietly overwhelmed.

The presence of all three indicates that it is most likely a Sunday.

I choke, cough, and hack down my breakfast, spewing food. Nephew wheels me to the living room. Stone, Mr. Bell, and Nephew situate me at my normal place on the couch. Nephew wipes my mouth, which contains bits of masticated food. Nephew also removes my soiled bib. The skinny, white guy seems to watch most of this in immobilized awe.

Stone begins, "Brother Rahja, this is Addison. He's beginning his mission work. He'll be with our church for another week. Then he'll be on to his next missionary post."

"Oh yea. God's gonna put 'em ... God's gonna put 'em in a good spot," Mr. Bell adds with a warm, comedic smile.

"Yes, precisely. Addison, this is Rahja." Stone formally introduces us.

Addison extends his hand nervously. Nevertheless, something rings deep within his awkward disposition, something deeply human, something deeply meaningful and simply prevailing. His grip is firm to my frail hand. As our eyes meet, a quiet pause seems to settle over my living room.

Stone continues, "Addison, why don't we begin?"

"Sure. Yes, of course," Addison says as though caught off guard yet happy to be centered with purpose. "The first reading is one of my favorites. I'm sure you'll recognize it straight away. It's from the book of Corinthians, chapter 13, verse 4: 'Love is patient ... love is kind.'"

I drift to some sort of thoughtless contemplation. The spoken words resonate within me. It's a place that reminds me of water. I can detect a calming. Their meaning and my ability to understand are no more than childlike. I continue to be delivered to a deeper and simpler place of peace. In my mind's eye, I can see the infinite expanse. I can see the beaming white sunset. I am lost in its glow. I am consumed in its brilliance. I am contained in its peace. I am beset by the power of the holy Word.

I look to Stone in an effort to center myself in the room. Our eyes meet. The depth and simple sparkle of his eyes sucks me in again. I can see the frosty white light of the eternal expanse in his eyes. I can see eternity in Stone's eyes. It seems more closely present in my living room. It seems the veil has been temporarily and miraculously lifted for just a moment. I become aware of Stone's eyes again. He smiles warmly and winks. Does he see it, too? Does he know?

"Mr. Bell, will you help us continue, Mr. Bell?" Stone asks.

"Oh yes," Mr. Bell says after a moment. It seems Mr. Bell has also been lost down the annals of his own reflection. Did he see it, too? Has Mr. Bell been captivated, too? Has he been captivated by a snapshot of eternity? Mr. Bell begins, "I'd like to talk about love, too, Brother Rahja. My reading is from the book of Romans, chapter 12, verse 9: 'Love must be sincere. Hate what is evil; cling to what is good. Be devoted to one another in brotherly love.'"

As Mr. Bell continues, I drift again to a most sensible place of peace. I close my eyes. Something about this whole scenario seems utterly ridiculous. I feel a sense of shame or embarrassment about the whole thing. Yet the company of Stone, Mr. Bell, and the new young man named Addison creates the most serene, completely simple feeling of contentment. I can surrender. Behind my closed eyes, I can see the fleeting memory of our family walks in the small town of Luck, Rose, Junior, and I just walking. I can see the barbershop marquee spinning. I can see Junior's fresh curiosity as his little finger points from his stroller. As I look to the eyes of my sweet wife, Rose, I can see the spinning reflection of eternity in her eyes. We just smile ... knowing.

Mr. Bell has finished his reading. Addison and Stone are conversing about some sort of parallel between Adam and Eve and Jesus and the Virgin Mary. I want to hear more, but the conversation carries them right out the door.

"Thank you, Brother Rahja."

"Yes, thank you, Rahja."

"Nice to meet you, sir," says Addison.

"I'll see you in a couple days, Brother Rahja," Stone says as he exits.

And just like that, they're gone. Once again, as usual, Nephew and I keep a vigilant watch over the house. As though all at once, the house is quiet again. It's void of persons and company. It's void of fun conversation and lively debate. A sense of connection is lost. Maybe it's something else ... some very basic aspiration. I am again in the grips of a lonely quiet.

"We'll be having lunch soon, Dad," Nephew says. I think he feels the sense of emptiness, too. Maybe he wants to keep the air filled with the ambience of conversation.

"Yes," I say.

As I begin to focus on the television screen, the telephone jangles. It is startling. Nephew answers. "Hello. Hey, Junior. Yes, yes. Well, you know. Stone was just here."

It's my son! He is on the phone with Nephew! It's my son, Junior. Oh, I don't know? How am I supposed to feel? I yearn so badly for my flesh and blood ... my only son. He was lost to me for so many years. And now he is within reach. But he is a world away. Well he's damn near forty years old. He's got his own life now. But I don't care. I want what I want. I'm anxious. My insides feel tight and uptight. What do I want anyway? I want an ending. And I guess I have that. But ... I ... it's more than that. There is more to it. There is more to the story, isn't there?

Nephew's conversation with Junior continues over the phone. "Yes, yes. Yes that sounds nice."

I am only privy to Nephew's side of the phone conversation. I wonder if I'll be able to talk to Junior. I am becoming less able to talk on the phone. Sometimes Nephew puts the phone on speaker. The supranuclear palsy has made it progressively more difficult for me to speak. I ... there are just so many things to say. There are still so many things to do.

"Dad," Nephew says as he walks with the phone. He's activated the speaker feature and continues. "Junior, Junior, are you there?"

"Yeah. Hey, Dad. Dad, how are you?"

"I ... I am doing all right."

"Well good. Ah, well listen. I'm gonna try to make it to your house sometime, sometime this week."

"Yes, yes do that."

"Well do what Nephew says to do. Take good care ... and—"

"I love you, son."

"I love you, too, Dad."

The call is over. It all goes so quickly. I think there is more. I think there is more to say. There is so much more to say. There is more I have to tell him. But time is running out. My time is running out.

Chapter 20

I choke down my lunch. I am deposited back to the couch. I'm exhausted. The phone call with Junior wore me out. It took only a minute, but it wore me out. I'll just shut my eyes. I'll just shut my eyes for a moment. I am soon fast asleep with the ambient background babble of the television. This sleep is different. These dreams are different. What are these messages? To what can I look to understand this connection? Who can I ask about these messages? I dream fitfully through the entire afternoon.

I can see folded notebook paper. It's got the ruled, light blue lines and the shredded remains of being ripped from a spiral ring binder. I unfold the notebook paper. It seems that the more I unfold it, the more there is to open out. The creases and layers just keep presenting themselves. I can see writing. It's handwriting. It suddenly occurs to me. This is a letter from Junior. This is the first letter I received after our estrangement.

After the divorce from Rose and the bungled visitation attempts, Junior and I lost contact. We lost each other. We were separated for more than ten years. I now hold his first letter to me after all those years. Why can't I open it? The layers of writing are getting closer. But I can't get to them. I feel frantic. My sense of frustration is mounting exponentially. I feel so close. It's right here in my hands. Yet its message remains locked away. As I begin to cry, my tears begin to soak the notebook paper. The letter turns into mushy papier-mâché'. It disintegrates between my fingertips. I just continue to shake and convulse with tears, watching and feeling the message melt between my fingertips.

I become lost and consumed in my sorrow. For a time, that's all there is. Then I become aware of a yellow light. As I focus on the yellow light, I become aware of varnished wood grain. As my focus becomes more distinct, I can see that the wood grain is worn and blemished. I lift my head. I am seated at a bar. Junior is seated next to me. We are at a rundown, dilapidated beer and whiskey joint. Other patrons are here, too. My tears continue to flow. I am ashamed and embarrassed. I am apologizing to Junior for having been gone all those years. I cannot tell if he understands my words. Then he looks directly into my eyes and face. He's speaking. But I cannot make out what he is saying. He puts a hand on my shoulder and leans closer to me. He's talking too quickly. The manner of his message is becoming more adamant. I am fading into tears and frustration. Junior is trying to tell me something. The sense of urgency becomes overwhelming. The energy in the barroom is mounting. The surrounding conversation is getting louder and more rambunctious. The crowd has grown considerably. Junior's face is edgy. The intensity is mounting to a degree I cannot endure. I begin to weaken. I feel I am growing faint.

Near that moment, a great silence breaks. Everyone quits talking. The jukebox stops. Particles of weightless dust float along the layers of thickening silence. Junior's face softens into a warm and welcoming smile. Everyone looks at me with care and understanding. I am the center of attention. I am the focus of the entire barroom. Then Junior performs a smooth and seamless somersault over the bar. His body doesn't seem to touch the surface of the bar. He disappears behind the bar. The noise of the bar recommences. The patrons go on about their business of drinking. I sink my head back to the bar.

After a period of blackness, I find myself lying on a cot. I am at home in South America. I am in a basic room on the ground floor. The room is painted a light green. The paint has faded considerably. Two windows are apparent, as well as a doorway. The windows and door are merely open-air apertures. They contain no screens or any means of adjustment. I am in a typical tropical rainforest dwelling. A small gecko scurries up the wall. The lush vegetation outside the windows is thick and luxuriant. Fresh drops of precipitation sparkle through sneaking shafts of sunlight. The smells and colors are especially vibrant and specific. I notice a sense of peace and rejuvenation. I am at the start of something. Perhaps I've been resurrected.

After a time, Junior stands in the doorway. He wears a loincloth and carries a ridiculous imitation spear. He looks to me. I look at him. For a moment, it seems as though the mood could become darkly serious or clouded with depression. Then we both laugh with such bliss and gladness. I feel a sense of youthful health. I feel glorious delight. Junior smiles and indicates that I follow him. He exits the doorway and disappears into the other-worldly vegetation of the rainforest. I follow quickly. Despite my haste, I lose him. I am struck with a quick sense of panic.

Then a dark, dirt path appears before me. It is beautiful. I immediately relax. It occurs to me that time no longer matters. I am outside of time. I am merely a thread in the eternal moment of time. The trail is all I need to concern myself with now. I know the trail will take me where I need to go. The trail will lead me to Junior. I begin to walk. Everything is so easy. I examine the multiplicity of plant and animal life as I stride. Everything is so sharply specific, faultless, and varied. I wonder about Junior. I am excited to see him again. I smile as I imagine him in the loincloth. It strikes me as comical and fun; so seems everything. I continue to steer and navigate the trail. Even though I am not finding Junior, I remain unconcerned. Then the trail ends. I come to a cliff. The sense of space is vast, infinite. The sky is never ending. I look out into a great expanse. There is not another side to the cliff on which

I stand. As I look out into the sky, I am aware of the soft, frosty, white-lit horizon. A beam of light stretches across the sky. It occurs to me that I am dreaming. In my dream, I realize that I've seen this before.

I wake up.

Chapter 21

Making peace with Victoria grew more arduous and complicated for Pauly. Perhaps the turbulent history they'd created together was what compelled it to continue. Their love for each other was not uncertain. Nevertheless, the relationship they shared looked to be fueled by dependence and dysfunction. One may also question the notion that part of their attraction to each other may have been driven by the misguided course in which they were engaged. Was it a lost dream? Was Pauly secretly wishing to be married and have a family? Was it lust? Did Victoria have the capacity for being truly committed to love? Was she seeking an unholy alliance? Perhaps they were motivated by the curiosity of their own corruption, a corruption with which they'd become intimately betrothed. It was difficult to say and likely ever-changing.

The bishop continued to visit the little northern town of Morningstar. Over the course of some years, a provocation came to pass. If things didn't change between Pauly and Victoria, Pauly would be asked to leave Morningstar. He would be assigned to another parish. Or he would be asked to leave the Church. Pauly wasn't asked to decide then. Nevertheless, in due course, Pauly would be obligated to make a choice, or a choice would be imposed.

He presented this to Victoria. She was aghast. She was unreasonably irate. Their relationship was certainly difficult for each of them. It was likely more complicated for her. It had gone on for years. Victoria grew more convinced that Pauly would leave the Church. He could then legitimately marry her. They could then lawfully begin their life together. She'd grown unwell both physically and mentally by the sham they played.

Pauly, on the other hand, was relieved by the Church's ultimatum. In his heart, he knew the Church was right. He knew the complicated knot that their relationship had assumed needed sharp and decisive action. Could the knot be loosened? Could the knot be untangled? Could they be unbound in a way that would provide a new course for each of them?

As it turned out, a priest in the city of Revelation Falls was soon to retire, and Pauly was offered the position. It was several hours away from Morningstar. It was a much larger parish and would likely provide Pauly with the fresh start he needed. He accepted.

He was split by his decision. While he was excited by the onset of this change, he knew the news to Victoria would be devastating. To his astonishment, it was he who was surprised.

He broke the news as softly as he could. Victoria paid less than full attention to what he said. She acted as though she already knew. "Yeah, I figured as much," she said. "You think you're ready for a change? Well I'm ready for a change, too. And you know what else, Pauly? You're not just getting away from me, not that easily. I can move, too. And you know what? I've already decided. I'm moving to Revelation Falls. Stanley's already got a job, and quite honestly, most of the kids are old enough to begin entering college. Revelation Falls has a great state college. You might not marry me, but, but you won't just be rid of me ... not after all we've been through together."

Chapter 22

It's late in the evening. It's near Nephew's bedtime. He's quietly watching television, folding laundry, and tidying up. Nephew is very efficient.

"Dad? Dad? Hey Dad ... listen ... ummm ... you slept almost all day again."

"Yes. I feel reasonably okay."

"Do you have any pain?"

"No, I ... I don't think so."

"Well listen, Dad. Auntie Rose called while you were asleep. I didn't know maybe, maybe I should have woke you up, but she uh ..."

As Nephew continues, thoughts begin to develop in my mind. I haven't talked to Rose since our divorce. That was over thirty years ago. Had we shared any words since then? Had we been in any sort of contact? I don't think so.

"Auntie Rose would like to see you. I didn't know what to say to her, Dad, but she, she's coming tomorrow."

What? Rose is coming here? Tomorrow?

"What?" I say.

"I hope that's okay. I didn't know what else to do. She was pleasantly insistent. I—"

"Yeah, gosh, okay. What time?"

"Tomorrow afternoon."

"Okay."

~

I don't know if I slept or not. My thoughts are disconnected dreams. Or maybe my dreams are disconnected thoughts. I'm anxious. I'm subconsciously unaware. I'm not able to settle. I'm not able to settle into any deeper currents. My thoughts race. I can't get a bead on any of it really. My emotions are mixed up with my thoughts. Maybe my thoughts are mixed up with my emotions. I keep trying to find a peaceful place. I take as deep a breath as I can manage. My body trembles at the uneven passage of oxygen. I try to find a solid place on which to hold. I try to locate a thought or an emotion that will impart some sort of restful revelation. I want some stillness. I want a sense of permanence, if only for a time. On this eve, it doesn't seem to be. The eternity of night stretches on. I close my eyes. I open my eyes. I remain in the grip of inner mental ramblings.

I watch the darkness of night make its imperceptible transformation to daylight. Morning still comes. I realize I am finally able to find a sense of centering in watching this simple event occur. I find my peace in the awareness of daybreak.

Nephew descends the stairs and begins our morning routine. He seems surprised to find me awake. Maybe he understands. We exchange no words. I think we are both anticipating the arrival of my first and only wife, the mother of my first and only child, Junior.

A Poem from Rahja to Rose

To be in love is a wonderful thing.
E're the thoughts of doth pleasure bring.
Remember, love must always be true,
Even when life tends to make you blue.
Sons of God were made to love
Evermore for the Father to see from above.

Love lightens labor so they say
Only if we learn to forgive and obey
Verily the Lord will one day say
Ever your days will be merry and gay

"You know, I haven't seen Auntie Rose for ... well since I was a little kid. It's got to be ... well I was still in South America. I was just a little boy when I first met Auntie Rose. I think Junior was just a baby. It was your first trip back home as a family. It was Auntie's and Junior's first trip home. Wow!" Nephew trails off, consumed in his own thoughts.

I finish my breakfast. I wait for Nephew to deposit me to the couch. But what? What's this? Nephew wheels me to the foot of the stairs. I am startled with bursts of anxiety. Nephew sets me at ease.

"I think we ought to get you upstairs for a nice shower and shave." Nephew helps me stand from the wheelchair. I put my arm around his neck. He takes a firm hold of my cotton waistband. From our entwined position, we embark the staircase, one step at a time. We slowly and steadily make progress. The consequence of each step brings hesitation and fatigue. It also brings a sense of vindication and victory.

The bathroom is the first room at the top of my staircase. The bathroom has become old and in need of a comprehensive cleaning. The carpeted floor is slightly soiled but a comfort to my bare feet. It's also warmer than the other rooms of the house. Its warmth is a result of how the ductwork is run through the walls of my house.

Nephew helps me out of my cotton sweat clothes. I'm naked, but I don't feel cold. I begin to feel uneasy again but say nothing. I begin to feel concerned about how I am going to get into and out of the shower. The sides of the bathtub are higher than what I'm capable of stepping over. Normally, I am merely given a simple sponge bath on the couch or before I am set to sleep. I can feel my heart begin to race. My breath quickens. My thoughts chase each other.

With Nephew's help, I turn and begin to move toward the bathtub and shower stall. A full-length mirror hangs on the bathroom closet door. I glimpse myself in the mirror. The image stops me in my slow-moving tracks. The moment is enigmatically majestic. I don't recognize myself. I know it's me. I am familiar with how I look. But how can this be? Is this my body? Is this who I am? My skin retains its supple, slightly toasted tan. I am East Indian, after all. I see an old man. I see an expiring old man. Wiry, gnarly hair sparsely adorns the usual locations on my body. My appendages have become whittled to spindles. My belly is abhorrently rounded. Without my dentures, my face is drawn and exhausted looking. I am feeble and weak. I look to my eyes in the mirror. I can't seem to get past their threshold.

Nephew brings me to the moment. "C'mon, Dad. Lift your leg. I gotcha. Here, put your arm around my shoulder. Put your weight into me. Now lift your leg."

I have one foot in and one foot out. I straddle the bathtub. I feel awfully susceptible. My body shakes. Falling down seems inevitable. The permanent sliding shower door prevents me free, open movements. Thoughts of losing my balance and falling down in the tub buzz loudly in my brain. I am aware of the hard, cold, unforgiving surfaces.

"C'mon, Dad," Nephew encourages.

Nephew maintains hold of me and maneuvers his way into the bathtub. He gets behind me and supports my torso, while I lift my other foot over the bathtub threshold. While I remain in his arms, he backs me up and seats me in the shower chair. I feel exhausted from the mindful exertion. Not to mention the physical effort, of which I am no longer fit. I am relieved to be seated, but my relief is mired in the thought that at some point, I'm gonna have to get out of here. The surfaces will be wet and slippery.

Nephew begins by shaving me. The shaving cream gives off such a wonderfully spicy aroma. The tug of the razor against my overgrown stubble is an appealing sense of resistance. I look to Nephew's face as he works on mine. His eyebrows and lips are furrowed in concentration. I can smell Norrie's hair grease, dish soap, green curry, and perspiration emanating from him.

After a time, my face is freshly shaved. He clips the hair in my nose. He clips the hair in my ears.

Nephew breaks the silence by turning on the water. He adjusts the temperature and then lifts the spigot to run the water through the handheld showerhead. The warm water is a tease to my skin. It awakens my nerves. It seems to melt the flesh beneath my skin. What a relaxing, restorative sensation.

"Make it warmer," I say.

"It's pretty hot, Dad. Isn't it?"

"Make it warmer."

Nephew adjusts the water temperature. I want to feel it. I want it to be slightly too hot. I want to have the sensation of cooling down once the water is shut off.

Nephew uses the shampoo and a washcloth. He gives me a methodical cleaning. The smells and tactile sensations are delightful. It's ticklish and makes me smile. I am usually bathed a couple of times a week. I always seem to forget how fresh and rejuvenating the experience is. I can feel my body calm and loosen. My thoughts empty and fall to contented blankness.

Nephew rinses me free of soap and prepares to terminate the flow of water. "Run the water over my head," I say. "Just run the water over my head for a little bit." I close my eyes as the warm water washes over me. The balmy and affectionate sensations dance over my skin. Something of me washes down the drain. I feel purified. I feel transformed. Nephew moves the stream of water from my head to my back. I open my eyes. Nephew is smiling. I am smiling, too.

My body feels weak and limber from the heat and humidity. I close my lazy and heavy eyelids. I feel a sense of disproportionate space and vertigo, but I don't care. The combination of sensations is such a delight. I just want to float. I just want to remain in this swampy sense of weight.

"Whoa, Dad ... Dad, you're falling."

Nephew's voice was already far away. I'm probably passing out. I can feel the gentle force of Nephew's arm across my chest, attempting to break my fall forward. The awareness of his arm reestablishes my sense of relationship with space. The sense of vertigo is gone. I am clearly falling forward. But it's too late; the vision has already taken hold. I feel my head clunk lightly against the bathtub faucet.

Padre Pauly and Victoria stand over me. How can this be? They're dead. I am still in the bathtub. They stand next to the bathtub, peering in through the sliding shower doors. Nephew is here, too, as well as some other bystanders with whom I am unfamiliar. I can see myself slumped over, face forward in the tub. I am unsure from the vantage point I see myself in the bathroom. The feeling is not one of urgency so much. However, there is a sense of restrained tension. Victoria and Pauly are talking. I can hear Victoria,

"Is it now? Are we supposed to show him now?"

"No, not quite. There is just one other thing."

"Oh well, he's certainly ..."

Then I can feel the cold, clammy sensation of my bathtub. The surfaces are hard and frigid. I can hear the water is still running. I can feel its warmth on my backside as the shower water washes over me.

"Dad, Dad. Geez, Dad. You must have passed out. Dad, you scared me. No more running the water that hot. Dad. Dad. Are you okay, Dad?"

"Yes, I ..."

Nephew sits me back up. I am groggy, but I am beginning to feel refreshed. He dries me while I am still seated in the shower. He dries many of the shower surfaces, too. He tends to the small cut and dimple of a bump that has developed on my forehead.

Chapter 23

Then the proverbial page turns, and I am placed back on the couch. I love the smell of the shaving cream and soap that I emit. I love the smooth fresh feel of my face.

Then a thought blooms in my mind. *Rose is coming here today. Rose will be here soon.* I am instantly astir with a jumble of thoughts and sensational sentiments. I don't know how to feel. I want to be happy. But what am I to be happy about? I want to be angry. I want to hide behind a stern, straight face. But what should I be angry about? More than thirty years have passed since I've had any sort of contact with Rose. Do I even know who is coming to see me? Do I know her? How can I say I know her anymore? I wonder to what degree I can claim to know.

Something inside me begins to wake up. It's been sleeping. I didn't know it was asleep. Something impenetrably deep begins to swirl within me. From this place comes a flood of flashes. An overpowering wave of recollections begins a slow march to the surface of my awareness. I can't let this happen. Such memories will have to be restricted. Otherwise, who knows what could happen. *Rose was the only woman I ever really loved. Junior was a pure and expressed product of that love. We were a beautiful family.*

I know I have to squash what is happening. I have to quash the electrical storm happening inside of me. This is too much. Rose and I will not be able to untangle. What is this about? Is this supposed to be about resolution? Am I angry? What does she want? What does she want after all these years? How dare her. But wait a second. I don't know. But I want to see her. I want to hear her voice. I want so badly to smell her.

The rush of thoughts is exhausting. The thickness and ambiguity of my tender emotions are too much to presently contend with. I drain my feelings. I try to put them in a hiding place. I don't want to find them anymore. I am tired. This is too much. How did I get here, again? I want to run. There is just no place to go.

A declaration has cropped up. The conclusion is becoming clear. Life has, after all these years, kept its promise to me. It's suggested itself to me as a solid relief. I know the depressed trench to which I have been relegated is exactly where I am supposed to be. I know it's dreadfully sad. I know this is not ending well. Hope's tunnel of light is growing dim, yet what a stable comfort. What a relief.

I close my eyes.

I open my eyes.

The picture window in front of my couch reveals the busy, urban backstreet. Over the years, the neighborhood has become less residential and more industrial. I can see busy Hmong people. They seem to be vastly assiduous. They seem to be good people.

Then a car pulls up. The car is tentative, as if checking house numbers. It parks in front of my house. Nephew comes down the stairs and announces, "I'm gonna take off for a while, Dad. I'll be back in about an hour or two." He proceeds through the kitchen and out the back door.

Through my front picture window it all unfolds as if in slow motion. Yet it's moving too quickly. Rose gets out of her car tentatively. There is a determined confidence within her decision to continue. She locks her car door and proceeds toward my house. She opens the front gate. She closes it behind herself. She has certainly aged. It's been decades since I've set my eyes on her. Yet for all that time, for that extensive absence, she remains the same. I can see the same college girl I fell in love with all those years ago. Her very essence is just as powerful as it ever was. Her physical form is merely the capsule that transports her beautifully perfect, untarnished soul. I am astounded. I am quite instantly filled with a feeling of the familiar. It settles over me and all the adjoining space around me. I am cast in a spell. I am cast in a spell I seem to know very well.

A curious thing happens to me as Rose makes the short approach from the front gate to the front door of my house; there is a very simple sense of understanding. I feel my anger give way to a much larger sense of tranquility. I realize any sense of resentment can never really gain foothold. The trivialities of ire or irritation suddenly become feeble, irrelevant, and sort of silly. The reason is simple. Rose sparked the fire. She lit the flame long ago. She illuminated the flare within me. I know that it can never be fully put out. It cannot be smothered. It cannot be stifled. There is a completely pure and untainted quality in its existence. But it's more than that. There is an eternity in it. It was only she who could have ignited such a light. Now that it's lit, it will always remain lit. Rose's soft pink firelight burns inside of me. These reflections happen all at once. I feel both uneasy and resolved at their notice.

Rose knocks on the door and enters my home. "Rahja?"

"Yes."

"Hi, Rahja. Wow, it sure has been a long time. Well don't you look good, Rahja. How do you feel?"

"I feel reasonably okay."

"That's good."

There is a glowing softness in our space. A tender and peaceful essence is shared but not explained. Simple words cannot provide clarification in this realm. It starts with the contact of eyes. Then it blossoms. The very shapes and forms of the physical world change. They change right before our eyes. But it's not surprising. This has always been the understanding, the expectation. The curves, contours, and soft slopes of her face change; they soften, they become more easily understood. A deeper comprehension is gained. The light switch on our souls has been illuminated.

Rose sits on the sofa adjacent to the couch. A weighty and consuming silence descends on the living room. The dust floats weightlessly in the rays of daylight. Rose looks around and seems to be settling into my living room.

"Rahja, what happened to your forehead? It looks like—"

"I bumped it this morning in the tub. It's no ... it's not really—"

"No, it doesn't look too bad. Just looks ..."

I don't really know what to say. I don't think she does, either. I concentrate on the babbling television. At some point, I make a decision. I decide to protect myself. I decide to protect myself and the flame that burns inside me. It is the flame Rose lit. I am glad and grateful for the flame. Any and all sensations are worth the weight and burden of the flame. I will bear such weight. I will carry the consequence. I will suffer the turmoil of knowing and the lucid comprehension of the simple eternity in the flame. However, Rose doesn't need to know, does she? How could I explain it, anyway?

"So how have you been, Rahja?"

"I've been ... essentially favorable."

"Rahja, I ... I just wanted to ... I thought it was time to—"

"Okay."

I'll shut it down. I've got to shut this down. No sense in opening any unnecessary doors. What is she trying to do, anyway?

"Is the TV kind of loud?"

"Nah."

"Would you like me to do anything, Rahja? Would you like me to get you anything?"

"I think everything is reasonably agreeable."

We continue to sit. Are the ripples or waves breaking through? Are awkward vibrations becoming apparent between us? But what do I care? Why is she here? What does she want? I am beginning to feel cagey. I want her here. I'm relieved, in a distant sort of way. But does she need to know that? What is she trying to do? I want her ... to be close. I want to feel simple intimacy. I want to smell her neck. Could I squeeze her hand? Could I give an offer of embrace? How can I do that?

"Can I use your bathroom, Rahja?"

"Yes. Either upstairs or right there in the hallway," I say, pointing.

She goes upstairs. I can hear the bathroom door close. The house falls silent. After a time, I can hear the internal plumb of rushing water. Then I hear the bathroom door open. I can hear her come out. She calls from the top of the staircase. "Would you like me to do this laundry here?"

"Nah, that won't be—" I answer, imagining the pile of laundry Nephew has left.

"It's okay," Rose answers. "I'll do it anyway."

She comes downstairs with the laundry basket between her forearm and her hip, just as I remember. I am hurt somehow by this simple memory.

"Is your machine in the basement?"

"Yes."

I can hear her descend the crooked basement stairs. I can hear the activities of clothes laundering. Soon she is back upstairs. She goes to the kitchen.

"Can I grab you something to drink, Rahja? Would you like anything? Ohh, is this curry chicken? May I?" she asks, becoming distracted.

"No, I am fine. You help yourself," I answer in anticipation.

Soon she's back, seated near me in the living room. She has a small plate of food and a Diet Fresca for each of us.

"Rahja, I ... I just want to know or understand that we can be ... okay with each other."

"Well I don't know if I could ever forgive you or ..." I say it meaning to be comical or to lighten the mood. But I know it's wrong as soon as it leaves my mouth.

"Oh, I ... well, Rahja, we have Junior and—"

"Yes, I ... you certainly did a wonderful job raising him."

"Thank you, Rahja, I ..."

The silence is all at once overshadowing and awkward. Let it be. I think about the flame. I think only about the pink candle inside of me. I think about protecting it. I think about the strange sense of urgency I feel.

"Rahja, I ... I'm sorry, Rahja. I ... I just wanted to ... oh ... I guess."

"Yes. I ... I just want to hold your hand ... or sometimes ... I ... or I mean ..." For crying out loud! What am I saying? My mouth seems to be working on its own.

The silence drifts into more silence. The space between our verbal melodies has fallen down again.

After a time, Rose gets up and returns her plate to the kitchen. I can hear running water and assume she is washing the plate. She returns to the living room and sits down.

"I'm sorry," I mumble. I feel angry and wish to be more openly sensitive. But this is her fault, isn't it? Why do I feel so provoked?

Rose nods with a most certain expression of knowing. I'd been entirely unprepared. I hadn't thought any of this through. I had expectations of control or some sense of masculine allusion. Instead, I find I am only lost. I feel no hope. It occurs to me that I may never see Rose again. I am most gravely staggered at the thought. I am consumed and shocked. I am only able to shut down further at the recognition of such dark entrails of deliberation.

I concentrate on the television in hopes of distraction. Perhaps it will serve as a hint for Rose to leave. But what am I doing? I can only hope that she will never leave.

"Rahja, Rahja, can I do anything for you?"

"No, I'm okay."

"Hey, you know," Rose begins as though legitimately excited about having something to say, "I understand that you quit drinking. Well some time ago. Is that true?"

"Yes," I said. "I just ... one day I just ... I couldn't ... I couldn't do it anymore. And ..." I didn't know what to say. I'd been defeated and devastated by the drink. I am suddenly irritated. Why did I not realize earlier in life? And now here sits Rose, long after it's too late.

Rose begins inquisitively although cautiously. "Do you remember Felicity Paul?"

"Yes, yes I think I do."

"Yes, she was the old woman. She was our neighbor, remember? She lived down the hall from us when we had our little apartment in Luck. Remember?"

"Yes, yes I do."

"Remember the evening she died? Oh, that was just so beautifully strange. She'd gone to the doctor for her routine checkups. I remember her telling me beforehand. She was so excited, or happy. I remember her being very serene. It was like she was preparing or ready or something. Anyway, that night, I had that wonderfully simple dream. In my dream, I sat up in bed. Felicity was there in our bedroom. She was standing over Junior's crib. Do you remember? Oh, how she used to love to look after Junior. Gosh, Junior would have been just over a year old at that time. Oh, such a strange experience. In my dream, I remember looking at the clock. It was just a few minutes past 5 a.m. In that dreamy state, I remember thinking; *I have to get up for work in a few hours.* I lay back down. I remember how peaceful I felt. The next day I got up and went to work. It wasn't until later that afternoon I got the call from Felicity's daughter. Remember? She told me that Felicity had died early that morning. Her daughter said she'd died just after 5 a.m."

Rose paused. She seemed deep in reflective contemplation and then added, "I knew something important had happened that morning, something simple ... something profound."

After a while, Rose departed. It seemed like she might have wanted to stay. But how could she have felt welcome in such debilitating environs? Maybe she'll write me a letter. Maybe Nephew will help me write her a letter? But no, I couldn't. But why not?

The pink candlelight that burns within me for Rose is enlarged and painful. I am consumed by its influence and imperiousness. It burns with strength and persistence. It burns with indifference and delight. Had Rose understood all along? Was Rose working to serve my suffering? Was Rose healing me? How did she know?

Nephew eventually returns. "Hey, Dad. You okay, Dad?"

"Yes."

"How was your visit? I tried to make it back sooner, but—"

"It was fine."

"Yeah?"

"Yeah."

"Okay."

Maybe Nephew can sense it. I don't know. This makes no sense at all. None of this makes any sense at all. This just doesn't make any sense. Or does it?

FROM THE DIARY OF ROSE
December 3, 2010

What a devastating crush. How painful. How difficult to see Rahja as such a fragile old man. I never imagined him as anything but strong. I know I ought not to feel shame or sorrow for him. But how? How to not feel sadness for him ... such complicated sadness. I wanted to stay. I didn't want to ever leave. Would Rahja surrender to my caring for him? It didn't seem like he wanted me there. I would have stayed ... then and there. I would have stayed until the end. My current marriage would have to wait. Would my husband understand? I could have. I would have. I would care for Rahja until the end of his days.

Chapter 24

Something within me changed after Rose's visit. I feel more deeply isolated yet freer. I feel shocked yet startled into a more centered place. I feel angry, yet my anger is curious. I know it's justified. But that makes no sense. My anger taunts and coaxes me into its mental ramblings. I glimpse my very inner recesses. I know that my soul is okay. Rose has mended my soul. I wonder if she mended my soul during her visit or in some other time immeasurable. Am I angry about her healing me?

The next couple days drift strangely; nighttime and daytime band together. Timelines occur, but they seem timeless. New things are occurring, but it's like everything has already happened in another time. It's all connected.

It is as though particular events are all timelessly bound within the simple flash of moments. I think about Felicity, how delightfully strange an occurrence. Why would Rose remind me of that? Why would Rose tell me that story again?

I go through my remedial routines. Nephew wakes me. I am provided all my daily rations of medications, insulin and otherwise. I am bathed occasionally. If I am not relegated to the couch, it is nighttime, and I am to be sleeping. Everything is drifting together.

Nighttime is sharp and vivid. When the time comes to close my eyes for rest, the brilliant ray of eternity is ever the more present. Sleep becomes a time of great light behind my closed eyelids. The blindingly soft light begins to bleed into my waking hours.

The degree of warmth and light are overwhelming, consuming, and intensely inviting. I am merely in their midst. Several things are occurring to me but in a way that I cannot explain. I am aware of myself in a way I cannot describe. I drift like a thread, attached to everything but not bound. I feel like a drifting ribbon, coiling and twisting around any product of my spawning. I feel like random wafts of smoke. Yet my movements are precise and perfect. Anything is possible. Anything is possible. Yet there is not anything to really do. I can do anything. I can manifest everything.

I can smell fresh linen. It has the most delightful smell. It's crisp. It's clean. Maybe it smells like warm apple pie. I can smell the whisper of a perfect flower. I can smell the immaculate. But these are bedsheets. The whiteness of their hue has a glowing effect. I lounge lazily. My head is under the covers. I am delightfully tangled in the sheets, but I am not aware of my body. Rose is here, too. I catch glimpses of her peachy skin. I reach to touch her. The intensity of the moment is suddenly amplified. She is here, but my touch is not realized. We both remain hidden in the glowing, white, silky-soft bedsheets.

The glowing white ambiance of the fresh linen bedsheets has been the eternal sunset. It's been the eternal sunset the whole time. This time, instead of being off in the distance of it all, I am a part of the light. I am the light. As I begin to ponder the simplicity and perpetuity. I become aware of the darkness. But I am no longer a part of it. I'm on the other side of it. I am in the light now. Who is responsible for this? Is Rose responsible for this? Is Junior responsible for this?

I feel the great sense of peace, simplicity, and eternity drifting away. I realize I am still appended or affixed by something. Some kind of a deep thought occurs to me. Someone is calling to me.

Chapter 25

Padre Pauly settled into his new parish. Because Revelation Falls was much larger than Morningstar, there were other priests with whom Pauly could associate. He liked the more current and contemporary feel of the city. He liked the diversity of opportunities. He liked the change of pace. He liked all the new people and places. He also liked the broken sense of routine from Victoria.

Victoria settled into her new home in Revelation Falls. She, too, was far more satisfied and rejuvenated than she thought she would be. She, too, was revived by a new sense of routine and change. She discovered unforeseen opportunities and became involved in ways she hadn't anticipated. As it turned out, Victoria's husband, Stanley, did not make the trip with her. It would mark the first event that would eventually lead to their official divorce. They'd already been separated for many years now. It was as though the marriage just went away. It disintegrated all by itself.

Eventually, Pauly and Victoria reunited. Without the presence of Stanley, their ability to share space went essentially unopposed.

<hr>

Pauly's first visit to Victoria's new home was ordinary. Pauly had constructed expectations in his mind. He foresaw the first meeting in Victoria's home to be awkward. It was very much the opposite. It was natural. Victoria assumed a rather nonchalant, indifferent demeanor. She was terse but accommodating. Her manner was cold yet suggestive. Pauly had forgotten how she could marry such normally disparate temperaments.

Victoria served coffee and homemade crumpets. Some of her children moved quietly through the home. They seemed cautious yet friendly and gracious. Most of them were either in high school or had already been enrolled at the state university in Revelation Falls.

Padre and Victoria sat quietly at the kitchen table. They shared relatively little in the way of conversation. Nevertheless, the moments were relaxed, comfortable, and without effort.

"Rose and Faith are soon to be enrolled at the state university," Victoria offered. "Some of the boys have started there."

"Yeah, that's great, Vicka."

"Well, would you like a tour of the new house?"

"Yeah, that'd be nice."

"Let's start in the garage."

"Okay."

Victoria led Pauly through the kitchen and into the garage. "It's not much to look at," said Victoria, "but I thought that may be a nice spot for you to set up a workbench."

"Oh, well, yes, I ..." Pauly was all at once renewed with a sense of apprehension and adoration.

"C'mon, Pauly, come in the house."

Victoria resumed the tour. "We won't go in the basement. It's all finished, but some of the kids are down there." Victoria led Pauly back through the kitchen and into the adjoining hallway. "There are more bedrooms down here, and here, here is Justina's room. Oh, oh my sweet baby girl, Justina."

The moment was suddenly filled with bulky and potent traces of suggestion. Pauly and Victoria shared a moment in locked eye contact. Their eyes sparkled. They both seemed on the verge of tears. Their eyes grew misty. However, no tears escaped the threshold of their eyelids.

"Pauly, you know she is going to be in high school soon. Can you believe it? Do you remember, Pauly? Do you remember when she was born? Oh Pauly. My sweet Justina, named after justice, you know. Because that was always my dream, Pauly ... justice. You know, Pauly?"

Pauly knew very well. As their affair gained steam so many years before, it was known that when Victoria had become pregnant for the last time, Stanley was not likely the father. The question of Justina's paternity had remained to this day.

"And here, Pauly, at the end of the hallway is my room. Here, Pauly, come look."

Victoria pushed open her bedroom door. As they passed the doorsill, she shut the door tightly behind them. They were back where they left off.

Chapter 26

"Dad, Dad. Better get up, Dad. Junior is coming today."

"Okay," I say.

My thoughts are plainly pessimistic. My thoughts are discouraged. Rose's visit left my heart feeling so heavy. It feels like Junior's visit will carry the same influential bulk. I don't know how to feel. I want to be happy. My only boy, Junior, is coming to my home. Maybe he will stay overnight. Will he stay? Such fruitless yearning is increasingly painful. Thoughts of his visit fuel cause for despair. My sense of longing for my boy feels complicated, gloomy, and tiring. I don't know. I just don't know.

Junior arrives early. I don't ever know when to expect him, but this time he seems early. Breakfast has been completed. I've been given my allotment of pharmaceutical chemistry. I am on the couch. Bob Barker and the Barker

Beauties are hocking game show ware on the *Price Is Right*. I think its Bob Barker. Who else would it be?

Junior and Nephew are on the front stoop. They're smoking. I can see them. Sometimes they laugh. I can hear them. The cigarette smoke smells good, but it teases the back of my throat, giving me cause to cough. I hold back the urge, fearing a full-blown coughing fit. Who knows? Water ... I could use some water. Sometimes Junior and Nephew look serious as they smoke and fall silent. Are they angry? What are they talking about?

Eventually, they come in.

"Water," I say. It comes out as a whisper. I don't want to start coughing.

"What, Dad?" Junior asks. "You need some water?"

"Yes."

He brings me a bottle of water. I gulp it. This is the wrong move. A good solid swig goes down my airway, and I heave and convulse. I can feel pressure behind my face as I pull for breath. I can feel my face turning red. My eyes fill with tears. My nose runs. Mucus and saliva splatter on the glass coffee table. The glass top was replaced about two months ago. I fell. It broke.

In due course, I regain my breath and composure. Nephew helps wipe my face and the coffee table. Junior helps to resituate me.

I am not feeling well. I don't know if it started with the coughing fit or before that. I can't catch my breath. I am hot. No, maybe I am cold. My heart and lungs seem to be out of sync. I have a strange nervous energy. Is this from the supranuclear palsy? I feel like I am sizzling in ice water. It's peculiar. I feel all at once in the center and far away. Junior and Nephew don't seem to notice. Junior eats a plate of food. Nephew tidies up the kitchen.

"Okay," Nephew says, "everything is set. Dad's lunch is in the fridge. You just have to heat it up."

"Is the insulin measured out?" Junior asks.

"Yup. Just give him the smaller syringe at lunch. He didn't really eat his breakfast, so the small injection should be good. "Dad? Dad?"

"Okay," I say. I am trying to gauge what is happening to me. My senses are all haywire. Everything seems to be on overdrive, but I can't get a bead on any details, or I can't focus. Is this anxiety I'm feeling?"

"Dad," Nephew continues, "I'm gonna take off for a while, Dad. I'll be back this afternoon. Junior is here."

"Yes, okay," I say with effort. I'm trying to gain some kind of mental focus.

Nephew leaves.

Junior and I sit. I am on the couch; he is on the sofa. The TV is like a clamorous and discordant chatty couple.

Junior and I are quiet. The TV is busy enough for the both of us. I feel a little better, but I still feel a sense of pain. I can't tell from where. With a bit of effort, I continue to focus. I am gaining a bit better sense of attention.

"Dad?"

"Yes?"

"Are you doing okay?"

"Ahh, not really. I—"

"Yeah, you look like you're a little uncomfortable. You look like you might be dizzy."

Junior and I have grown more settled over the past couple of years. I became reunited with him when he was twenty years old. He's almost forty now. How can that be? We're quiet now. It seemed in the earlier times of our reacquaintance Junior was frustrated. Maybe he was angry at me. Maybe he was annoyed at other stuff. He used to bring his girlfriends around. I miss that. There doesn't seem to be much to say anymore. But that's not true. Have we tried? Have we tried talking about ...? Is there a disconnection? But how to ... there's so much. Am I supposed to talk about his mom with him? Rose should have never divorced me. But then she did such a good job of raising him. But I'm his father. But can I say that? Can we pick up? Can we pick up after the mess we made? Can we pick up where we left off? But where did we leave off? He was just a little boy. How strange all this is. He is the little boy I didn't know. Now he's a man. That's the disconnection.

"Son?"

"Yes?"

"I love you, son."

"I love you too, Dad. Are you feeling a little better?"

"Well, I'm gonna rest for a while now."

"All right."

I close my eyes. I'm out.

Chapter 27

A gateway or portal is here. Right here in my living room. It's marked by a bright, brand-new barbershop marquee. It spins its eternal movements to the sky. It gives me a feeling of such simple joy. The marquee just quietly rotates its eternal movement. I can feel a sense of both laughter and tears cropping up within me. I am in my living room, but it seems brighter. The presence of light is peculiar. It's a kind of light that doesn't have an associated shadow. Then I hear something like the sharp and crackling snap of a gunshot. Wow! Something is vibrant and exhilarating.

Padre Pauly is here. He's driving his off-road truck. I'm bumping around in the passenger seat. One of Rose's brothers is with us, too. He rides in the backseat. His name is Chase. I think he was just released from his latest bout in prison. We're riding through a farmyard, past corrals that contain cattle and horses. Padre Pauly owns a small plot of hunting land among the rural farmland of central Minnesota. "The Forty," as it's called, is only accessible by passing through the bordering farmyard. "The Forty" refers to the forty or so acres of land Pauly's plot encompasses.

We meander along eroded and washed-out field roads in the four-wheel-drive truck. After a short drive, we come to a corrugated steel cabin and shed. Pauly parks and cuts the engine. We disembark. It's a bright and welcoming spring day.

I am confused by our purposes at The Forty. On one hand, our time at The Forty was often reserved for the deepening of our family relations. A strong sense of bonding and kinship was forged and renewed there. On the other hand, as Chase unloaded the booze and Padre Pauly handled the crossbow, I knew our reasons for being there were not entirely honorable.

As the vision of Padre Pauly begins to fade, I am struck by such confused and complex thoughts of him. He was such a generously warm and compassionate man. He seemed to wield a deep and simple way of wisdom. Just the same, he'd spent years as a hopeless alcoholic. He poached wildlife with an arsenal of illegal weaponry. His unusual involvement with the brilliantly corrupted ways of Victoria (Rose's seemingly wicked mother) always struck me as entirely out of his character. As the vision fades entirely, I am left with a thought: maybe Padre Pauly understood or contended with more than what met the eye. Why the contradiction? Why the unanswerable questions? He healed me. He healed my soul.

The vision deepens, but somehow becomes less specific. I am aware that my being is enveloped. My sense of being is wrapped by a soft yet immovable ribbon. The ribbon is my protection. The ribbon is my salvation. The ribbon is my treasured cosset. The ribbon is God. I realize it's always been there. Forever and always. I have always been inseparably interwoven with God.

Visions of Padre Pauly fade into visions of my mother. I can smell her. I see her dark, intelligent eyes. I feel a shade of her stern indifference. Her knowing presence remains silent to my uncertainty. A sense of soft forgiveness passes between us. But it's deeper than that.

Is that the sound of running water? Mostly it seems like flashes of light. The movement is fast, like lightning. Am I moving that fast? Is the space around me moving that fast? Is that the wind I feel? Am I in it? Is it in me? It's the connection. It's the conduit. It's the channel. It's the source. I'm not passing through it; it's passing through me. I get uptight. I try to relax. It's so beautiful. It's so delightfully and flawlessly sad. I feel I am being cleansed by my own tears.

All at once it stops. It is as though I float in the tranquility of embryonic fluid. I have an awareness of hearing, but I don't think I can hear anything. I have a sense of smell. I can smell ... I can smell my mother. I can smell her breath. I can smell her perfume. I can smell the static electricity of her freshly combed hair. I can smell the perspiration only she emits.

I am in a tropical forest. Rays of warm sunlight shine through the thick upper canopy of overgrowth. Exotic noises busy the soundscape. The flora reveals a plethora of unexpected sentient color. I am aware of the shaded, moist earth below me. I know it's moist, but I cannot feel it. I move with purpose. I have a sense of where I am going, although no particular trail guides my path. I move with curiosity and optimism. I navigate the rainforest as though I know exactly where I'm headed. Is it familiar? Have I been here before? I come to a thick patch of soft undergrowth and plant life. A small creek runs past the threshold of the floral wall. The water babbles quietly. The water babbles a tender anecdote.

A small boy kneels alongside the water's edge. His head is down. He examines the ground beside the running water. He concentrates with intent. Then he throws a pebble into the running water and looks toward me. I realize the little boy is me. Our eyes are gently engaged. He walks toward me and takes my hand. We don't speak. We don't need to. Subtle understanding transpires between us.

He walks me into the babbling brook. As we enter the water, I realize it's surprisingly cold. It has no shallows. It drops off directly. It drops to a bottomless depth straightaway. I falter and begin to panic as I tread water frantically. I sink. I open my eyes. A white beam of fire-like light shoots through the water. The heavenly beam goes on indefinitely. The beam of light shoots in both directions for farther than I can see. It is well below my submerged position in the water. I can see the little boy—my young self—is swimming below me. He's swimming toward the white source of light. I begin swimming toward it, too. I realize the flaming beam of indefinite white light is Rose.

Then it all seems to wash away, like a big funnel. It's like an enormous whirlpool. I begin heaving. I feel like I'm choking.

Chapter 28

After some years, Pauly retired. He conducted some remedial assignments with the Church, but for most intents and purposes, he was done.

He eventually settled in permanent residence with Victoria and the children who remained in the home. It was difficult to determine with any degree of precision how Victoria's children felt about Padre Pauly. They seemed to accept him. There were even times in which warm regard and true affinity seemed to be exchanged. After all, several years of history had developed. Just the same, as they were older, Victoria's children had also developed a sense of the dysfunction, corruption, and insidiousness that had in many ways become their norm.

While relations with Victoria's children remained mostly lukewarm, Pauly did develop some more substantially well-knit relationships with a few of the boyfriends.

As Victoria's daughters grew, they entered the realm of dating. The nature or comfort of that transition could certainly be argued. Considering the example the children had been shown growing up, they were apt to hold to a wider array of questions, discomforts, and insecurities. Nevertheless, over the course of time, the daughters began to bring young men around. One young man in particular made quite an impression on the family and Padre Pauly. His name was Rahja.

Victoria's daughter Faith had initially brought Rahja home for a family dinner. It was an awkward evening but nothing extraordinarily far from the norm. From the beginning, it was clear that Faith and Rahja's relationship would not likely grow to anything more than a friendship. They were companionable classmates. However, it wasn't long before Rahja and Victoria's other daughter Rose began an unforgettably passionate and turbulent path of simple adoration and love. It burned rather brightly but for only a short time. Yet its pink flame would never be fully extinguished.

Chapter 29

"Dad."

I wake up foggily. It is becoming more difficult for me to breathe. I can't tell if my condition is getting better or worse.

Melody is seated in the living room with Junior. Melody is a lady friend. We worked together for some years before I retired. A relationship of sorts developed between us. She and I have a basic way of meeting each other's needs. She doesn't come around much anymore. It's strange to see her. But then again, it seems apt. Melody has a way of showing up at just the right moment, when least expected.

They both look toward me with concern.

"Dad?"

"Rahja?" they both chime in. It has a synchronization that seems like a joke. Did they try to do that? Are they aware of the harmonious coincidence? Their expressions of concern do not change. They must not have noticed.

"Dad?"

"Rahja?"

I try to answer. I only cough. I am aware of my attention toward breathing. It is rather difficult. Is it supposed to be this labored? My breaths are short and quick. It feels like someone tunneled out my lungs and filled them with wet gravel. It's strange. The gravel isn't moving, but a little air is still able to get through.

Melody and Junior discuss options. "I wish Nephew were here," Junior says.

"Is this normal?" Melody questions, "Should we call an ambulance?" When is Nephew going to be back? Should we wait?" Is there a pill we could give him?"

Then the doorbell rings. Junior answers. An unfamiliar gentleman follows Junior back into the living room. He wears a shabby suit. His face is sloppily shaved, and his greasy hair seems slightly pasted to his scalp. He is in need of a haircut. Although I can't smell him, I imagine he smells like salted onions. The unfamiliar gentleman and Junior converse with each other.

"Yeah, he's pretty sick. He seems to be having a pretty bad day," Junior explains.

"Right, well, as long as he is awake."

"Okay."

"You can hold the pen for him, and help him sign."

"Okay."

Junior and the unfamiliar gentleman approach me. "Dad," Junior begins, "this gentleman is a public notary." Junior then produces a crisp multipage document. "Dad, this is an updated power of attorney. It gives me equal power to make decisions on your behalf. It's ... it will supersede the last one. If you could, would you be willing to? Here's a pen."

Junior holds the document before me and places a pen between my static fingertips. Some indication hangs in the air. Time hangs in the quiet, brimming with anticipation. Electricity seems to wax and wane unpredictably. Expectation seems a sharpened #2 pencil.

I sign. I have no problem with that. Did they think I wouldn't? The stillness in the living room settles to something new. The unfamiliar gentleman stamps the power-of-attorney document and takes leave.

The stillness in the room remains. My breathing still feels like it's going through wet gravel.

"Do you think we should call an ambulance?" Melody continues.

"I don't know ... Dad?"

"Rahja?"

"Should we call you an ambulance, Dad?"

"Rahja, should we call an ambulance?"

Melody and Junior talk. They talk about me. I guess they're talking to me.

"Rahja?"

"Dad, should we call an ambulance, Dad?"

"Yes," I say. "That would be okay."

A general tension takes over the living room. Activity ensues. Junior is on the phone. "Hello, yes, yes, my dad needs an ambulance. No, I don't know. He's having trouble breathing. Yes … no … okay … okay."

Junior hangs up the telephone. He asks Melody, "Are you leaving?"

"Yes, I think I'm gonna leave."

"I wish you would stay."

"No, I don't like this. I don't like to see Rahja like this."

"I think you ought to stay."

"No, I need to leave."

Melody comes to me. She bends over. We are face to face. I can smell her chewing gum in bursts of her warm breath.

Her difficulty in speaking scares me. I can smell the perspiration and perfume of her skin.

"Rahja, Rahja ... you take it easy. They're going to take good care of you. I'll come to see you soon."

Melody leaves. I wish she would stay.

Chapter 30

On the surface, Padre Pauly and Rahja had little in common. Padre Pauly was a retired Catholic priest from a small northern town near Canada. Rahja was an international student from somewhere in South America. How they came to cross paths in Revelation Falls was certainly curious.

Their time together was sporadic at best. They obviously led very different lives. Yet when they did share space, it was evident they were kindred spirits. One such occasion is worthy of mention.

The Forty was a forty-acre plot of hunting land a short drive from Revelation Falls. It was surrounded by farmland.

Padre Pauly had initially purchased a portion of the land sometime midway through his career in the clergy. Near his retirement, he inherited a neighboring share. The Forty was a getaway. It was a hiatus, an oasis. Pauly often invited people to The Forty, usually one or two at a time. Much of the activity was focused on hunting, hiking, and other outdoor endeavors. He had a small garden there. There was a small cabin on the plot, as well as a large shed that housed a tractor, ATVs, and other motorized implements of tending the land. Not long after attaining the plot, Pauly very much understood The Forty to be his simple slice of heaven.

The Forty had an ominous side, too. However, as the nature of that darkness was explored, one may question to what degree goodness was able to prevail. The delineation of right or wrong may never be entirely discernable.

Rahja was already pretty well drunk. Amusingly, Pauly had all but ended his longstanding business with the sharp amber nectar of inebriation. Rose's brother was also there on this occasion. His name was Chase. He'd just been released from his second stint in prison.

The men approached the cabin on foot. Rahja stumbled on the uneven ground in the controlled way that only an experienced drinker could. Chase walked a quick, side-by-side route, seeming to explore all the freedoms of his recent release from prison.

The men gathered at the cabin deck. Pauly and Rahja sat, letting their feet suspend above the overhang. Chase continued to pace. He wore an enchanting and entertained smile. Rahja hung his head. It appeared to be the gesture of the distraught. Pauly and Chase observed Rahja with neutral detachment and then looked at each other.

They had brought a small duffle bag of simple provisions, a dangerous-looking crossbow, and a small case of assorted liquor. Pauly took hold of the crossbow with an easy dominion. He took quick aim and sent a short, stout arrow flying with ferocious velocity into a tree stump some thirty yards away. The precision weapon emitted a tight, contained snap as it released the trajectory. The arrow wisped through the air with a quiet lethality. The simple sounds got Rahja's attention. He looked up sluggishly.

"Gimme that," Chase commanded with a charismatic smile.

Pauly handed it to him, along with a small quiver of arrows. "Take it easy with that thing, Chase. And easy with those arrows, and—"

"Yeah, yeah, yeah. I know what to do. I'm gonna go kill something. Ha, we'll fry it up. You can cook small forest animals, can't ya, Padre? Or Rahja, you can cook it, can't ya?"

"Just be careful, Chase, please," Pauly pleaded. "And try not to lose any arrows."

"Yeah, just be ready to cook something. I'm hungry."

Chase took the crossbow and walked swiftly toward a wooded trail in the back portion of the yard. The day was climatically tepid. The sun warmed. The breeze cooled. Chase entered the wooded trail and vanished into the forested path. A drying swamp butted up against the wooded portion of the yard. Cattails blew slightly with the breeze. A bird or two made quick pit stops along the flowering tops.

Rahja looked up. His eyes were comically and sadly unfocused. Pauly looked at him with paternal concern and stark impartiality. "Once you sober up, Rahja, we can get us a deer."

"Pauly, it's not even hunting season. How can you ...? Ur, I mean how can you? That's not really legal, right? I mean, you."

"Not to worry, Rahja. Nothing will be known or wasted ... and ..."

They sat quietly for a time. The quiet between them transformed to the sounds of the scenery. Birds sang broken melodies. The wind grew and receded through the trees and brushy countryside. It was as though the natural environment infused in and through them. Or maybe they became infused within their surroundings.

After a time, Rahja began, "Oh, Pauly, man, I, ah ... I gotta talk to you. I, Rose is pregnant, and—"

"Well, well. Congratulations, Rahja. I've often thought you and Rose make such a wonderful couple. I am certain you will represent fatherhood very well, Rahja."

"Yea, but shit, Pauly, I, ur, I, I'm still having a problem securing my citizenship. And I have to get a respectable job. And oh, Pauly."

"Let me tell you something, Rahja, that stuff doesn't matter one iota. It's inconsequential. It's not important. That stuff will work itself out just fine. It might seem like a big deal now, but listen to me, Rahja, it's all going to be just fine."

"Yea but—"

"Rahja, all you've got to do is keep taking good care of Rose. Son of a gun, Rahja, you're going to love that little one when it's born. You're just going to love being a father, and Rahja, promise me you'll be careful with the drinking, huh?"

"Yeah. I, I'm just so—"

"Let me tell you something, Rahja, let me tell you a little something."

"Okay."

"This is important, Rahja. I want you to listen to me well. Someday you'll pass this on. Someday you'll pass this on to that little one you have coming. Okay? So hear me now, Rahja, listen now to what I am going to tell you."

"Okay."

"You remember those old barbershop marquees? You know, the kind that spin? Yes? You know how they have that stripe or that ribbon that wraps around them? You know how the ribbon spins over the length of the spindle? It creates an illusion. The stripes appear to be traveling up the length of the pole rather than around it.

"Yes? Think of yourself as the spindle, Rahja. Think of the ribbon or the red stripe as God. You get it? When you look at the ribbon on the spindle, you can never see the entirety of the ribbon at any given angle. Yet it's always there, Rahja. It's always connected. It encircles us. It never becomes separated. It's whole. You can't always see it. You can't see all of it, but trust it, Rahja. It's always there."

Pauly paused and looked at Rahja. Rahja sat looking more lucid, with reflective speculation. Rahja had an unburdened, faraway look on his face.

Pauly continued. "Did you know the red and white barber pole used to represent something having to do with bloodletting. The spinning marquee was a representation of bloody bandages wrapped around a pole. During medieval times, barbers performed surgery on customers, as well as tooth extractions and who knows what else. The original pole had a brass washbasin at the top, which symbolized the vessel in which leeches were kept. The bottom signified the basin in which blood was received. The pole itself represented the staff that the patient gripped during the procedures to encourage blood flow.

"Isn't that something? I do enjoy that history, but the analogy pointing to God seems a nice way to understand something quite simply. It makes better sense to me."

"Yeah, wow, Pauly. So you're saying that the spindle is a symbol of me, and the stripe or the ribbon, like on a candy cane or on a barbershop sign, can be like God? Yeah, yes. I like that. Thank you, thank you, Pauly."

"Go lie down for a bit, Rahja. When you get up, we'll go and get us a deer."

"Okay."

Chapter 31

A fire and ambulance crew arrives. Junior lets them in. They're burly, aggressive, and loud. They assume control. They take command. They have questions. "What's going on here?" "Where is he?" "Can he move?" "Can he walk?"

Are they talking to me? Junior does the explaining for me. I lie on the couch and watch all the happenings around me. Everything seems to be so all at once. It's miserably exciting.

The emergency personnel come prepared with an array of portable appliances and implements of primitive and other than natural healing. They lift me from the couch. They use the sheet that I've been lying on as an application of transport. They carry me outside in the bath sheet, using it like a hammock. I am cradled like a baby into my small urban yard. They put me down on the ground and then lift me onto a gurney. Is this really happening? Again?

The situations occur in flashes. Another ride in an ambulance. This is like a dream ... maybe it is a dream.

It's an earful of sirens. But no, it's not sirens. It's the singing of songbirds. I am afloat with birds. There are so many. Birds of an infinite variety float around me. They welcome me. Birds as diffident as the hummingbird and majestic as the great condor are all flying around me, swooping and gliding along. Their colors are vibrant. I am so happy to be flying. But I wonder if I am flying. But yes, something extraordinary is happening. It is as though I am blasted by a slingshot. I'm flung. I realize I am no longer attached. Anything is possible. I feel a sensation, like an expansion. I am stretched. I am stretched to the possibility of limitlessness. Glorious quintessence and burst understanding are now known. It is like a selfish and boundless inhalation ... to the ends of the universe. The inconceivably infinitesimal is also known. I am free. I am unattached. A simple serenity dawns.

Then I am trapped by dimness. I am trapped in its shadow. The form of shadow becomes more specific. A clattering of noise and a sense of urgency is known. Bright, synthetic lighting ... and fear ... and ... panic. Stainless steel and limitations inhibit my environment. I am aware of my body ... from afar. Then all the pain and discomfort. All the terror and depression jolt me. Those in medical garb surround me. Their eyes are shielded. Their mouths are covered. I am on my back. They surround me with tubes, tools, and the archaic implements of stainless steel healing. I don't know if I am in my body or not. My body and soul are not joined properly. The surrounding medical personnel seem determined in the midst of their hurried and panicked actions.

Then another jolt ... like lightning ... like the blast from the barrel of one of Pauly's shotguns. It is beautiful. This is it. This is where I am from. This is providence. But I come to know the timing isn't right. Everyone is here. They're telling me the great story. This is the great gathering. The joy ... the bliss ... the simplicity—it's like everyone always says but infinitely superior. It's far simpler. But I can't really stay. Not yet. However, the destiny is made plain. It makes sense. I already know what I have to do. Can it be explained? Is it simply beyond words?

I wake up in the intensive care unit. This scenario has played itself out several times. Tubes and beeping appliances encircle me. I feel the pain and hiccups of my worn-out body. I feel almost entirely used up. Nephew is here. Junior is here, too. They're talking with one of the nurses.

"Yes, it's quite remarkable," the nurse says. "In fact, I don't quite know how to explain it." Junior and Nephew pay close attention as the nurse gathers her facilities and continues. "There is a protein in the heart muscle called troponin. When someone has a heart attack, troponin is released into the body. In other words, as portions of heart tissue begin to expire, they're released into the body. Troponin can be detected for several hours after the episode. Normally, if the level of that protein is below .15 parts per million, the patient is generally conscious. Any number of tests can be run. The patient usually responds well to medical intervention. Of course, other circumstances come to play. Your dad," the nurse said, addressing both Nephew and Junior, "had levels over 10." She paused, allowing the information to permeate. "But that's not even the most astonishing part. Your dad had a second heart attack that we were not aware of. I, I don't know how he could have survived. He's been the talk of the unit. He obviously has quite the constitution."

Times have become just plain grim. I know it unambiguously. My soul knows it, too. All the same, a certain peace floats up from somewhere, a substantial and encompassing sense of calm.

I feel less attached to my body. It doesn't really work anymore. It hasn't actually worked for a long time. I'm sad, yet the emotional part of me is also beginning to fail. I am losing my physical capabilities of communication. I can't talk. My mouth and tongue seem to work sloppily at best.

It's a confusing time. It's an awkward time. Yet the sense of shame or embarrassment I used to feel about it doesn't seem to jab me at me like it used to. I don't feel the sharp electricity of those particular feelings. Those around me don't really know what to do.

I am introduced to a feeding tube. There seems to be a good bit of controversy surrounding the implementation of this device. I guess I don't see the big deal. I know my time in my body is short. It is difficult being unable to talk. I have become a better listener. I am not used to that.

From the hospital I am moved. I am excited to go home. But they won't bring me home. I am brought to a rehabilitation hospital. I think this is where people are brought to die. I don't mind the place, but I want to go home. They continue to work me with the feeding tube. It seems a good deal of apprehension and disagreement surrounds the use of this device. Several heated conversations are held. I am aware of these things in a way I cannot fully explain.

Eventually, they take the feeding tube away. I am relieved. But what can this mean? They try to feed me through my mouth. But my mouth doesn't really work anymore. All of this has such depressing connotations, but somehow, it isn't entirely gloomy. I'm just tired, peacefully. They all try talking to me. It's pretty nice.

Chapter 32

At long last they bring me home. What a simple and precious gift. Returning to my home holds such significance. Although seemingly plain and basic, pulling up to my curb and front gate in the hospital transport van is deeply powerful for me.

I remember the day with a keen sense of clarity. I remember how the wind blew. The day was overcast and gray, but it wasn't dark. It was bright. The overcast sky was frosty and white, with a low, swiftly moving, puffy layer of clouds. The temperate and heavy wind seemed to carry the potential of moisture and volatility. It howled through the buildings of my urban neighborhood. It whispered loudly through the trees. It came through the walls of my house. Yet the space of my home remained hushed and motionless. The wind came into my body. It moved through me. It was light and ticklish. The wind was. The wind just was. Its message was strong. Its voice was clear. It was a tempest flurry. It was with me. It was in me. It was me. It was an exceptional zephyr.

***

A new bed has been placed in my dining room. It is equipped with a morphine drip and an oxygen reservoir.

These were illuminated times. But can I say that? The light shone brightly into all the living spaces of my home. Is it the light of eternity? Its luminescence is without shadow. This is the light of eternity. The end is near. Yes, the beginning is near. I am in my home. This is it. This is finally it.

People come to visit. It's strange to see these sad people. I know all of them, but I haven't seen them in such a long time. Why are they coming now? Why are they so awkwardly distressed? Do they know why they're sad? They look at me with such longing. It seems I am only acting as a mirror for them. They seem to be consumed with all their own issues and the bits and pieces of what they have yet to resolve.

They miss it. I think they're missing the point. The secret is right in front of them. They're a part of the secret. The light is everywhere. They're the light, too. We all are. We are all the light. It's implausible, yet so ordinary. It's like Plato's fireside allegory. The white eternal sunset is coming to get me. The everlasting horizon is swelling and expanding to engulf me. It will be here soon. It's coming to get me. I wonder if the others can see the wave. Yes, I know they can.

Padre Pauly is here. I can smell him. I can smell the brand of cigarettes he smokes. He stands quietly at my bedside. His face carries the same soft smile. His presence and quiet wisdom settle my soul.

I've been at home for about a week. I am on my deathbed, as they say. I'm waiting on death's bed. I am waiting to be free. I seem affixed to my body. It is as though I am unable to die just yet. The bouts I experience out of my body are now happening with permanent frequency, yet I remain attached to my body and this world. I wonder why. But I know why. The answer reveals itself in the question. It seems I've come to the crossroads of a contradiction. Perhaps our struggles and trials are just a simple masquerade. Perhaps the tribulations we've embraced have only been those which we've accepted. Perhaps they are only those we've been familiar with. Perhaps they've been the very things we've yearned for. Is that why we've come here? To resolve the problems of our choosing?

I know love exists. Junior is proof. Rose and I made him. Junior is love. Rose and I made him that way. It's pretty simple.

It could not be any clearer. I've come to understand why I've hung onto this broken body so long … all these debilitating years. I no longer eat. I no longer speak. I am no longer mobile. My left eyelid now only droops.

Nephew is not here this morning. Nephew is not at home. Junior is here; my only son. Junior is in the house. I can sense him here. I can sense Junior's presence. He's in the house. Today is Junior's day to watch over me. Nephew is gone. Nephew went to church. It's just me and Junior today, me and my boy. It's me and Junior today—my very own flesh. My very own blood. Today is the day I die. By order of the cosmos, Junior and I forged a union in his creation. Junior and I will again embrace this union as I take leave behind the curtain. I will finally exit this ailing and delicate body. It's going to happen soon.

Is Junior ready? Is Junior ready for this? Am I ready for this? I'm ready. I think Junior is ready, too.

It's bright outside. It's bright in here, too. The sky is overcast. Yet the illuminated quality remains. It's been like this ever since I got home from the hospital. These bright, cloudy, windy qualities. The universe seems a bit worked up. The pinnacle, the apex, the acme is near. The universe has apparently prepared extraordinarily well.

It's all swirled up. It's a tempest of elemental forces. It's been planned with artistic precision. It's euphoric with an easy gladness. Yes, an exceptional zephyr.

I am aware of these things ... *all* of them. I can see my fragile and fading body. I can see myself lying on the hospice bed. I can see my pale, physical self.

But I'm seeing these things from above. I float. I can see these things from somewhere above. I can see Junior. He looks to be sleeping. I float to him and cross his handsome threshold. He's cast in the grips of a wonderful dream. It's a dream I enter. It's a dream we can share. Padre Pauly has also been kind enough to join us.

Oh, how the wind blows. The lovely wind.

We just dream ... and ... dream together.

We can see it all in such detail. And we can see it all at once. In fact, we've always seen things this way. There has never been any other way.

The light ... the light is completely and perfectly bright. This light is imminent and prevailing, without shadow. This is the true essence. This is how. This is simple and everlasting genesis.

But, that means—that could only really mean—well, then.

The wind, the wave, everything is swirling so beautifully. Everything is perfect. Everything has always been perfect. The wind ... the waves ... the wind and waves are building. The energy is becoming concentrated. The concentration has a purpose. The concentration is with deliberation and universal vision. Its lens is focused on the entirety. This is a singular vision. This is all there is or has ever been.

Padre Pauly is telling us the story. We can see him. But it's more than that. We sense his entirety. He's telling the story again. He is telling it to Junior, too. It's the story of the barbershop marquee. Pauly is explaining it again. Our essence together is combined ... intermingled. The essence of we. We are being wrapped in the ribbon of God. We are the combined essence. The ribbon is God. Is Junior getting this? Does Junior understand? Is Junior getting the message? Yes, yes he is. The seed has again been planted. The message will take root. The message will grow. The message can now blossom.

I am no longer attached. I am no longer tethered to my body.

From above, I can see Junior. He is coming to my body. I am no longer there. He's looking at me. He stands close to it now. He bends to place his cheek against my open mouth. He knows now. He knows a piece of it. He's leaning over me. He touches my forehead. He kisses it. He tries to shut my mouth. It's frozen open.

Finally! Finally, the wave crests. The wave crests and takes me with it.